The Silverlake Stranger

This book is for Tim and Deb
with much love; and with
appreciation to Honey Rock
Camp and Camp Timber-lee,
who provided those wonderful
weeks at summer camp!

The Silverlake Stranger

Sally Marcey

Tyndale House Publishers, Inc.
Wheaton, Illinois

Books in the Choice Adventures series

1 *The Mysterious Old Church*

2 *The Smithsonian Connection*

3 *The Underground Railroad*

4 *The Rain Forest Mystery*

5 *The Quarterback Sneak*

6 *The Monumental Discovery*

7 *The Abandoned Gold Mine*

8 *The Hazardous Homestead*

9 *The Tall Ship Shakedown*

10 *The Class Project Showdown*

11 *The Silverlake Stranger*

12 *The Counterfeit Collection*

Copyright © 1992 by The Livingstone Corporation
All rights reserved

Cover Illustration copyright © 1992 by JoAnn Vargas-Weistling

---

Library of Congress Cataloging-in-Publication Data

Marcey, Sally.
    The Silverlake stranger / Sally Marcey.
        p.   cm. — (Choice adventures ; #11)
    Summary: The reader's choices control the adventures of Jake, who
unwillingly goes off to a summer church camp that turns out to be more
interesting than he could have imagined.
    ISBN 0-8423-5048-9
    1. Plot-your-own stories. [1. Camps—Fiction. 2. Christian
life—Fiction. 3. Plot-your-own stories.] I. Title. II. Series.
PZ7.M32824Si   1992
[Fic]—dc20   92-36889

Printed in the United States of America

99   98   97   96   95   94   93
 9   8   7   6   5   4   3   2   1

Jake spotted the ugly yellow bus waiting in the small parking lot of Capitol Community Church. "See ya," he mumbled as he slid out of the passenger seat of his aunt's car.

"Have a wonderful time at camp, dear," his aunt called after him.

Jake muttered something in reply. He couldn't believe he was going to church camp. He ducked his head and rapidly crossed the street. In the church parking lot, he saw a few 14-year-old kids clustered around Pastor Whitehead, talking excitedly.

Jake shook his head. He hoped none of his friends from the city would ever find out he was here. They would never be caught dead doing anything with these geeks.

And I wouldn't have to be here either, Jake thought to himself, *if it weren't for the Vipers.*

The Vipers!

Jake remembered the night when his best friend, Johnny Rogers, had told him excitedly, "The Vipers are going to let my brother Ted join their gang! He gets to go with them tonight. Wanna follow 'em?"

Jake had shivered inside. He knew he was tough, but even he hadn't wanted to get messed up with the Vipers. But he couldn't tell Johnny that. So he just shrugged and said, "Yeah, sure."

2

He and Johnny had trailed along behind Ted just to see what the Vipers were going to do. They had stayed out of sight as Ted had met Bill Grossman and some of the other members of the gang in an alley behind a grocery store. The group had talked a few moments in whispers, and then they had moved out. Jake and Johnny had struggled to keep up.

When Bill paused in front of a drugstore and pulled out a gun, things had started to get serious. Jake's hands got clammy just thinking about what had happened next. He could still see the gun handle in Bill's hand crashing down on that storekeeper's head!

Jake shut his eyes for a moment to clear his thoughts. The worst moment had been when Bill had raised his head, glanced through the window, and looked right at Jake!

"Get that kid," Bill had growled. Jake and Johnny had run then, as fast as they could, and dashed into a deserted building. The police sirens wailed a few moments later. The Vipers hadn't been caught.

Two days later, Jake's aunt had called to invite him to spend the summer in Millersburg. "Jake will enjoy the change of pace from the city," she had promised Jake's dad. She hadn't mentioned church or church camps. Jake hadn't known then whether to be angry about leaving his friends for the summer or thankful to be getting away from Bill Grossman, but it had only taken him two seconds to decide to go.

"Still, camp wasn't part of the deal," Jake grumbled. He caught sight of the wildly gesturing hands of the youth leader from Fairfax Congregational, Jeff Ellers. Jake winced. What a loser! He was so tall and gangly that he couldn't even get through the youth group meeting last Sunday without tripping during one of the games and knocking over a can of soda. This was really going to be some week.

When Jake reached the group, he put down his duffel bag and tried to blend in without calling too much attention to himself. He thought he had been successful—until Jeff spotted him.

"Hey Jake! Good to see you here!" Jeff elbowed his way through the group, bumping into a few kids in the process, and clumsily patted Jake on the shoulder. "Great that you could make it!"

"Yeah, great," Jake mumbled, trying to avoid Jeff's overeager smile. How uncool could a guy get?

"I want you to meet some of the guys from Capitol. You already met the ones from Fairfax last week. . . ."

"Was forced to," Jake muttered under his breath.

". . . but the guys at Capitol are really great and . . ."

Jake stared at Jeff. He narrowed his eyes and without saying a word shot Jeff a look that said, "Leave me alone, you're acting like a jerk." Jeff reddened a little and backed up a step. "Well, maybe later would be a better time to . . ."

Jake deliberately turned his back on the youth leader, picked up his duffel bag, and casually walked away from Jeff and the chattering group of kids. He had circled the bus and started to move toward the bus door when he glanced sideways and noticed the alley behind the church.

Perfect, he thought. *If I slip into the alley, no one will*

4

miss me for a few minutes. Everyone will think I'm on the bus. That'll give me enough time to hitch a ride back to the city.

Jake shivered. Maybe he should lay low this summer and go to camp after all. But then he thought of spending a whole week miles away from nowhere with a bunch of spastic kids.

If Jake decides to run away, turn to page 41.

If Jake decides to get into the bus, turn to page 53.

Jake didn't move. Steve's outburst was like a seven-year-old's challenge to bullies, a sermon, and a mother's lecture—all rolled into one. A few minutes ago Jake saw Steve as a do-gooder, one of those have-it-all-together types who make guys like Jake feel like losers. Suddenly Steve seemed more human. He didn't just want to reform Jake. He cared about Jake, and not because he was better than other people, but because he really believed in Jesus. Jake decided to stay and listen.

Steve looked down, shaking his head. "I just hope you're not going to be the stranger this week, Jake. I like you. You seem like a decent guy—like you might listen to Jesus. Yeah, you're tough, but not hard like some of the guys I've seen. Not like the ones who lead gangs. Well, if you're set on flushing this week down the toilet, then I guess nothing I say's going to change your mind. But I don't think you're that far gone, and I just wish you would at least be fair and give God a hearing, even if I am being obnoxious by saying all this."

Jake stepped back in the cabin, closed the door, and leaned against it.

Steve continued, "I don't care if you don't fit in with the younger kids or if you can't swim or if you don't like the woods, Jake. And I don't know what else I want to say except, just loosen up. At least come to the meetings and

6

listen to the messages. You don't have to sit in the front
row or play stupid games. Just give God a chance. He's got
nothing against you. This week is a great opportunity to
hear what he has to say. No back allies. No gangs. No
guns. No graffiti. No noise. No lies." Steve stopped. He
knew he was impulsive, and he was afraid he'd already
said too much.

A few more seconds of silence went by. "OK," Jake
finally said.

Pause.

"OK what?" Steve asked.

"I'll help you out."

Steve nodded. He picked up his screwdriver and
handed it to Jake. "All right." Steve waited for Jake to say
more, but what he had already said, and done, was a giant
leap forward. Steve knew that, so he didn't push it.

Steve cleared his throat and began to explain what he
was doing with the outlet. Jake nodded. The two worked
together the rest of the time until supper. As they worked,
Jake told Steve about Bill Grossman and the Vipers and
what had happened at the drugstore. Steve listened
patiently.

"By the way," Jake added as they were cleaning up, "I
don't think I can give up smoking all week. I've tried
before, and . . ." Steve said he understood; he agreed to let
him smoke outside the cabin and the dining hall.

"Jake, there's one more thing I should say."

"What's that?"

"It may be a few days before the other guys trust you.
I think you're going to have to win them over."

Jake nodded. "I think I know what you mean."

Steve smiled, and they made their way to the dining hall.

A good week was underway.

Turn to page 70.

8

I'm going to follow him," Chris said matter-of-factly. He got up and headed in Jake's direction.

He quietly followed Jake into the woods, taking care not to be seen. Finally Jake sat down on a log and opened his hand. Chris was surprised to see a pack of cigarettes in Jake's open palm.

"Satisfied?" Jake sneered without turning around. "Going to run and tell Steve or Jeff?"

Chris jumped. "How did you know I was following you?"

"I could hear you breathing," Jake stated coolly as he lit a cigarette and inhaled slowly. "Boy, you guys make me sick. Always sneaking glances at me when you think I'm not looking to try to see what I'm doing. And now, following me."

Chris was about to deny Jake's words. Instead, taking a deep breath, he decided to tell the truth.

"You're right. We don't trust you. I was following you because there have been some things missing in our cabin—"

"And right away, you think I'm the one who took them," Jake interrupted angrily, turning around.

"I did," Chris admitted hesitantly, feeling a little sheepish. "But Jess thought we should give you a chance."

"What? Jess thought . . . ?" Jake growled. "You guys really like talking about me, don't you?"

"Sorry," Chris said slowly. Then he deliberately looked Jake straight in the eye. "Did you take anything from our cabin?"

"Maybe," Jake taunted. "Maybe I did."

Suddenly Chris blurted out the thought that had popped into his mind. "You don't want us to like you."

"What?" Jake looked startled.

"I think you don't want us to like you, so you deliberately do things to keep us away," Chris continued, thinking out loud. "Maybe you're even taking things to make us mad at you."

Jake just stared at him. "You're nuts," he snarled.

"But who has been taking our stuff, if you haven't?" Chris asked. "I think I'm going to talk to the other guys again to see if they have any more ideas. See ya, Jake."

Jake watched Chris head back toward the cabins. Suddenly he remembered the bearded man who had asked him to go fishing the first day of camp.

"Hey Chris!"

Chris stopped and turned around.

"The first day of camp, I fell asleep in a clearing by the path in back of the cabins," Jake began. "When I woke up, this strange man was watching me. He asked me to go fishing."

"So?"

"I didn't trust him."

"Jake," Chris said impatiently, "you don't trust anyone. What was his name?"

"Nate Sares."

Chris shrugged. "I saw him at the boathouse with Steve. He's some sort of outdoorsman. I don't think he's our thief."

Chris headed back toward the cabins. Jess was waiting by the rock.

"Well, is Jake the thief?" she asked.

"I don't know," Chris answered. "But I think we'd better call a meeting for all the Ringers after breakfast. We can meet in the clearing in back of Cabin 8."

"Should we ask Jake to come too?" Jess asked.

"No way," Chris said. "I'm still not sure if he's the one."

CHOICE

Turn to page 62.

You guys go ahead. I'll meet you at the bridge," Chris called over his shoulder as he waded toward the bank.

"Watch out!" Sam yelled. "That guy's tough."

Chris vaulted out of the river and began to jog through the woods the way Jake had gone.

Without warning, someone jumped him from behind. Chris's arms were yanked back. "Looking for me?" Jake's voice growled in his ear.

"Yeah, I don't like guys bad-mouthing my friends." Chris twisted around, breaking Jake's hold, and sprang free. Half crouching, he faced off against Jake.

Jake laughed. "Where'd you learn to fight?" he snarled, watching Chris weaving around him, "sissy school?"

Chris sprang for Jake's legs.

The two of them went down and began to roll around on the ground. Chris grunted as he tried to get some leverage against his heavier opponent.

Jake twisted in Chris's grip, hitting him whenever he could. Chris tried to dodge Jake's fists as he strained to trap Jake in a wrestling move.

"You shouldn'ta called Willy a name," Chris said as they struggled.

"Why not? He's black, isn't he?" Jake countered, finally rolling on top of Chris.

12

"Willy's my friend," Chris grunted, struggling to get free.

Jake's fist hit Chris's face. Chris winced under the pain. Blood streamed from a gaping cut above Chris's eye.

Chris twisted around, reversing their positions, and jumped to his feet.

"Had enough?" Jake growled, panting.

Chris wiped the blood from his face and said, "No, actually, this is great practice for wrestling," trying to sound nonchalant.

"Maybe so, but don't you guys think it'd be smarter to save your energy for canoeing?" Jeff Ellers was smiling at Chris's remark as he stepped through the trees. His smile faded abruptly when he saw the blood on Chris's face and Jake's angry expression.

"What's going on here, Chris?" Jeff asked sharply. "What happened to your eye?"

Chris looked at Jake standing there sullenly. Now was his chance to get Jake in trouble. He straightened up. "Ah . . . Jeff, . . . Jake and I were fighting—"

Jeff looked at Jake, who was larger and obviously stronger than Chris. "Fighting about what?"

Chris hesitated. Suddenly he wasn't sure he wanted to get Jake in trouble. Wasn't a Christian supposed to show mercy?

Jake broke in. "I said something stupid. Chris popped me. I popped him back. He lost. Case closed."

Jake's admission shocked Chris so much that at first he didn't know what to say. Finally he nodded and said, "It's OK, Jeff. It's no big deal."

Jeff looked slowly from one boy to the other. "OK," he said skeptically. "The bridge is only two miles downstream. You guys think you can get there without killing each other?"

They both nodded.

"All right," said Jeff, not completely satisfied. "Take care of that cut, Chris. I'll see you *both* back at camp."

Jake waved and smiled.

"Thanks, Jeff." Chris turned and began walking toward the bridge. Jake followed him. Jeff watched them both for several minutes.

"Thanks for saying you said something stupid," Chris said when Jeff was out of earshot.

"Don't mention it," Jake said sarcastically.

Chris was wondering what to say next when Jake said suddenly, "Race ya to the bridge!" and began to run.

Chris was so surprised that Jake got a good head start before Chris even started running. Chris could see some of the other Ringers watching them by the bridge. He sprinted as fast as he could, but he couldn't catch Jake. Panting, Jake reached the bridge first. Chris was just behind him. Together they collapsed on the bank by the river.

Jill and Tina walked over to stare at them.

"What happened to your eye, Chris?" Tina asked.

"We were wrestling," Jake said. "Chris lost."

"Did Chris teach you some moves?" Jill asked innocently.

"Yeah," Jake dead-panned solemnly. "He was teachin' me how to wrestle."

Jake looked at Chris and both of them started to laugh.

14

"Boys can be so weird," muttered Jill as she and Tina walked away.

Chris and Jake just kept on laughing.

THE END

Turn to page 121.

I've got to follow Jake! Chris suddenly decided, and he dashed back into the cabin. Ripping a page from his notebook, he quickly scratched a note to Jim. "I hope Jeff doesn't talk Jim's ear off," Chris muttered as he dropped the note onto Jim's bunk.

Chris crashed out of the cabin door once again and into the woods. He followed the trail until it forked.

Wonder which way they went? he thought. Then he noticed something on one of the paths. *A cigarette! It must be Jake's!* And he plunged down the path.

After running for a while without seeing any sign of Jake or the thief, Chris began to have his doubts. *Great,* he thought. *Now I'm not sure which way Jake went. Jake could already be in trouble.*

Chris stumbled over an exposed root across the trail and almost fell. Just then an arm shot out from the under-brush and grabbed him.

Chris reacted instinctively and started to wrestle with his attacker.

"Chris, ease up, it's me," hissed Jake.

Chris stood up slowly and helped Jake to his feet.

"I thought the plan was for you to get help," Jake said sarcastically.

"I was worried about you," Chris said. "I thought Nate

might have seen you following him, and then you would have been in trouble."

"Not a chance," Jake scoffed. "I could hear you behind me for the last ten minutes. When I thought we were getting close enough to the thief for him to hear you too, I decided to stop."

"I *was* making a lot of noise. I can't move quietly through the woods like you can," Chris admitted ruefully. "Now what do we do?"

"I thought this was *your* plan," Jake responded.

"Well, I could go back to get help now. Or we could walk back to the cabins and tell Steve. What do you think?"

Jake hesitated, surprised to be asked at all.

Neither boy was aware that the thief was listening to them, concealed in the underbrush several yards down the trail. A nasty smile crossed his face.

"Let's stick with the plan, Chris," Jake said finally. Then he lowered his voice. "You run back to get help, and I'll try to find where the thief went."

"I don't know," Chris said uneasily. "It'll be dark soon. Why don't we both go on ahead?"

Jake just shrugged. "Suit yourself."

"How do ya walk so quietly, Jake?" Chris asked as they continued down the path. "I always make a ruckus."

"Don't know," Jake mumbled.

Unknown to them, the boys were almost to the spot where the thief was hiding. Jake stopped suddenly.

"What?" whispered Chris, alerted by Jake's taut stance.

Jake shook his head. "Let's head back," he hissed,

abruptly pulling Chris with him as he whirled around and began to jog back the way they had come.

"Hey wait!" Chris protested and twisted under Jake's grasp. At that moment, the thief crashed out of the underbrush behind them.

"Run, Chris!" Jake yelled, but the thief was too quick for them and grabbed Chris's shoulder.

"What're you boys up to?" asked Nate Sares, smiling at them.

"Let go of me!" Chris yelled, trying to struggle away from Nate's grip.

Nate kept smiling. "Not until you tell me why you were following me."

"We saw you take some stuff from Cabin 4!" Chris blurted out.

Nate released Chris and chuckled. "What stuff?" he asked.

"A couple cameras and a suitcase," Chris stated.

Nate turned for a moment and reached down into the brush beside the trail. He picked up his tackle box.

"Are you sure this wasn't what you saw?" he asked calmly. "I was going to try a new fishing spot. Johnny from Cabin 4 was going to go with me. I was just checking to see if he was ready to go. I had a couple of cameras with me to take some pictures."

"Ah, well . . ." Chris looked at Nate uncertainly. "Maybe we did make a mistake."

"No, we didn't," Jake said coldly. His eyes had never left Nate's face. "You're lying."

Nate's smile never wavered, but his eyes narrowed for

a moment. "That's a pretty strong accusation to make," he stated calmly.

"Maybe so," Jake muttered, "but it's true."

At that moment, Jim and Steve with the other Ringers rounded the bend in the trail and jogged into view.

"Hey guys, what's up?" Steve asked.

"Well," Chris began, "we were following Nate. We thought we saw him take a suitcase and a couple of cameras."

"We *did* see him," Jake interrupted. "Nate's the thief."

Steve looked at both boys, then at Nate.

"What happened, Nate?" Steve asked calmly.

The thin, bearded man told his story.

Steve listened without comment. When Nate was finished, he said, "Be careful when you accuse someone of stealing, guys. That's a pretty serious thing to do."

Chris looked sheepish, but Jake met Steve's gaze defiantly.

"However, Nate," Steve continued, "Johnny is staying in Cabin 7 this week."

"Musta gotten my cabins mixed up," Nate said with a shrug.

"And Johnny signed up for a trail ride today during free time," Steve continued.

"He must've forgotten about fishing. Well, I'd better be going," Nate muttered hastily.

"Wait a minute!" cried Pete, emerging from a particularly dense clump of bushes. "Look what I found!" In his upraised hand was a camera.

Abruptly Nate's smile vanished. He whirled around

and began to run down the trail. The Ringers started to run after him but Steve shouted, "Come back guys! Don't chase him." When the Ringers gathered around Steve, he said, "We'll go back to the campsite and call one of my friends on the police force. They'll get to Nate's cabin before he does."

"Why did you look for the camera, Pete?" Tina asked as the Ringers were jogging back to camp.

"I heard everyone's story and I believed Jake," Pete answered.

Jake took on a look of shock.

Jill laughed. "Well, you were right."

"I believed Jake, too," Steve added, "but I wanted to give Nate a chance to defend himself."

Jake shook his head. People didn't usually believe him. As he jogged beside the others, he suddenly decided to tell Steve about the Vipers. It would be a relief to tell someone what he had seen that night in D.C.

When they got back to camp, Steve called his friend, Officer Walker. Nate was gone by the time the police got to his cabin, but they did find many of the stolen articles from camp.

After breakfast the next morning, as everyone was getting ready to leave the dining hall, Officer Walker stopped by with the stolen things. The guys were glad to get their stuff back, especially since none of them had ever expected to see it again. It was a relief to all the Ringers, too—though none of them said so—that Jake wasn't the thief after all. In fact, on this particular day, it almost seemed to them as if he were more like their big brother.

20

Before they left, Officer Walker shook hands with them all and thanked them for helping. Jake stood there stunned. What a crazy idea—working *with* the police. It was the first time for Jake . . . and it felt pretty good too.

THE END

Turn to page 121.

Sam took a deep breath and began to swim toward the raft. He put his head down and swam as fast as he could, trying not to think about how deep the water was. Finally he reached the raft.

"Good job!" Jeff exclaimed, treading water beside him. "But Sam, you don't have to swim so fast going back. This isn't a race."

Clinging to the raft, Sam stared at Jeff.

He doesn't know how terrified I am of deep water! he thought as he caught his breath.

Sam pushed off the raft and began to swim as rapidly as he could back to shore. When he looked up to take a breath, it seemed as if the shore was still the same distance away! He put his head down and swam again. This time when he looked up, the shore still hadn't moved!

I can't touch the bottom! he thought, remembering the sinking feeling he'd had at the Coast Guard facility when he had jumped in the water and his life jacket had flown off. That was before he knew how to swim. Feeling the panic overtake him as it had before, Sam started thrashing about wildly, afraid of being trapped underwater again.

Immediately he felt a strong hand supporting him in the water. He heard Jeff saying calmly, "You're OK, Sam, just catch your breath for a moment. Roll over on your back and float."

Sam turned over onto his back and took deep, gulping breaths. He was shaking all over. Knowing that Jeff was treading water beside him really helped. Finally, he calmed down enough to flip over onto his stomach. He continued to swim shakily back to shore.

"Good job, Sam," Jeff said proudly, as Sam stood panting in the knee-high water. "It isn't easy doing something when you're afraid."

Catching his breath, Sam looked gratefully at Jeff as the other Ringers crowded around him to congratulate him.

Jeff continued with a twinkle in his eyes, "Even though you passed the test, Sam, I don't think you should swim to the raft alone."

"No kidding," gasped Sam.

"You'd better wear a flotation device when swimming out there, until we can retest you."

Jeff turned to the other Ringers.

"You guys all passed. You can swim during free time, as long as you always swim with a friend."

"Did you really beat Steve in swimming?" Chris asked, picking up his towel.

"Yes, but I never tried to wrestle him," Jeff said with a grin. "He was undefeated in that department."

"No way!" exclaimed Chris. "Maybe he can teach me a few wrestling moves this week. I really want to make the team next year in high school."

"Ask him, Chris. I bet he'll be glad to help you."

Jim laughed. "I'm with Jeff. I don't think Steve's someone I'd like to wrestle."

"Hey, here comes the next group of campers!" Sam pointed to the top of the hill leading down to the lake.

"I'm going to help them with the swim test, too. Why don't you guys take some free time before supper?" Jeff suggested. "We'll meet in front of the dining hall at six o'clock."

"Let's go, guys!" Willy exclaimed, and as they walked away from the lake, he lowered his voice and said, "I have an idea."

"I'll catch up with you guys later," Chris began, "I'm going to try and find Steve."

"Chris," Willy pleaded, "I've got an explosive plan!"

CHOICE ➡

If Chris decides to go with Willy and the gang back to the cabin, turn to page 50.

If he ignores Willy and decides to look for Steve, turn to page 92.

Let's try one more time to right the sailboat," Jim suggested. The three boys pushed as hard as they could on the dagger board. The sailboat started to right itself, but then sank back into the water.

"I have an idea," offered Pete when they had caught their breath. "Let's boost Willy up and have him stand on the dagger board. Then we'll shove down on it as well and try to push the sailboat upright."

"It's worth a try," agreed Willy.

"I'll count to three. On three, Willy, we'll boost you up." Pete counted, "One, two, three!"

The two boys hoisted Willy as far as they could out of the water. He scrambled onto the dagger board while Pete and Jim pushed down on it. The sailboat began to move.

"Keep pushing," encouraged Jim through gritted teeth. Inch by inch, the sailboat's mast righted itself.

"Yea!" Willy cheered, flopping back into the water.

The three boys managed to pull each other into the boat by using their weight to balance the boat. Just as Jim heaved himself into the boat, lightning crackled across the lake. The wind was gusting behind them now, pushing the sailboat farther away from shore.

"We'll have to tack," Willy shouted, grabbing the tiller, rain splashing against his face.

"Let's not try to get back to camp," Pete called out,

watching the lightning flash again. "Just head for the nearest shore, Willy."

Laboriously, the three boys zigzagged toward the shore, steering the craft against the wind. Finally, Jim jumped out of the front of the boat and dragged the sailboat onto shore. After they had pulled the sailboat out of the water, the three boys began to walk along the shore back to camp. Halfway there, the rain started to let up.

When they were almost to Camp Silverlake's dock, they heard a motor running over the water. Steve's blond hair could be easily seen in the graying light. Running toward the shore, Willy began yelling and waving his arms.

Steve caught sight of him and came around, heading into shore. They met him at the boat dock.

"We were worried about you guys. There's quite a storm heading this way!" Steve exclaimed. He vaulted out of the motorboat onto the dock. "What happened to the sailboat?"

As they headed up to camp, the boys told Steve the whole story. And later, after the storm passed, a truck was sent out to pick up the stranded sailboat and bring it home to safe harbor.

THE END

Have you met the Silverlake stranger yet? If not, turn back to the beginning and make other choices along the way.

Or, turn to page 121.

Willy maneuvered the canoe sideways in the current and pushed it several yards toward the shore. When the canoe bottom began to scrape in the shallows, Willy let go. Immediately, he swam back to the stream and started kicking as fast as he could with the current. Before he knew it, he was bobbing beside Jake. Jake's head was lolling to one side. His eyes were closed. Willy grabbed the back of Jake's life vest and kicked for the nearest bank.

He dragged Jake onto the shore. Once they were settled, Willy noticed Jake's eyes open and close slowly. He was conscious, but dazed.

"At least he's still breathing!" Willy thought out loud. "Now what'll I do?"

"Help!" he called. "Help, somebody!"

Behind him, the woods were silent.

Willy watched the stream, hoping some of the other canoers would be along soon.

"There's our canoe!" he exclaimed, watching it float toward them. "I'm going to get it." He plunged back into the stream. When the canoe floated by, he grabbed it and dragged it to the shore.

"OK, Jake," he gasped, heaving the larger boy into the canoe, "let's get out of here. We're lucky your paddle was tied to the canoe!"

Willy jumped into the back and began paddling hard downstream.

In the front of the canoe, Jake groaned. "Willy?" he asked dazedly, shaking his head. "What happened?"

"The canoe flipped over."

"I don't remember anything after we paddled past the tree," Jake said unsteadily. Then he leaned over the side of the canoe and vomited.

Willy remembered what his Red Cross instructor had said about bumps on the head.

"Jake, we'd better get help. I think you might have a concussion."

While he was speaking, Willy searched the sides of the stream for a small house or a boat dock. When the canoe rounded the next bend in the river, Willy spotted a small white house nestled between some birch trees back quite a way from the river. On the beach in front of the house, another canoe was turned upside down.

"Hope somebody's home," Willy said, paddling toward the shore. When he reached the bank, he jumped out, waded around to the front of the canoe, and pulled it out of the water.

Jake looked awful. Willy started to pray that someone would be in the house and that they would be friendly.

"I'll be right back, Jake," he said as he began to jog quickly toward the house.

He bounded onto the little front porch and knocked rapidly. When no one answered, he tried the door. It opened silently.

Now what? thought Willy. *Should I go in or not?*

28

CHOICE➤

If Willy decides to go into the empty house, turn to page 49.

If Willy decides to go back to the river and Jake, turn to page 120.

Jake decided to head toward the clearing. When he got there, he sat on a log to think. He was fidgety without his cigarettes, but he sure didn't want to return to camp. A long hike seemed like too much work.

He looked around at the ground by the log at his feet and saw a soft, springy carpet of moss. Bending down, he touched the moss with his hand and felt its softness. Gingerly, he lowered himself to the ground and braced his back against the fallen log. The sunlight was warm, but not too bright. *It's so peaceful in the woods,* he thought drowsily, and before he knew it, he was asleep.

Jake woke up suddenly. He knew, before he even opened his eyes, that someone was beside him. He opened his eyes and instantly rolled to his feet in a half-crouched position.

"Steady there, I'm not going to attack you." A lanky, brown-haired man straightened up from his slouch against a tree and smiled at Jake.

"Who are you?" Jake held his ground as he narrowed his eyes and stared at the man's bearded face.

"I'm Nate Sares. I own a cabin about two miles down this path. Are you one of the campers at Silverlake?"

Jake grunted in reply.

"I was just going fishing," Nate said. Jake's eyes flickered to the ground beside Nate's feet, where a tackle box and a couple of fishing rods were lying. "Want to join me?"

"No thanks." Jake spoke clearly this time. He didn't trust this man.

"Suspicious one, aren't you?" Nate commented, still smiling. "That's OK. It's not wise to trust someone you don't know. Well, I'd better be off. Tell Steve Barton hello from me."

Nate picked up his rods and tackle box and headed down the path toward the lake.

So much for being alone, Jake thought as he turned around and saw Jim Whitehead coming toward him.

"Who was that?" Jim asked, pointing toward Nate's retreating back.

Jake shrugged. "Says he lives in a cabin around here. Did you come to check up on me?" Jake asked sarcastically.

"No," Jim said with surprise. "Why should I?"

"Everyone else seems to want to," Jake muttered defensively.

"I'm going for a hike around the lake before supper. Wanna come?"

Jake shook his head. "What's with you guys? You don't seem to get it, do you?"

"Get what?" Jim asked, puzzled.

Jake muttered something under his breath, jammed his hands into his jeans pockets, and headed down the trail away from Jim.

Jim watched him thoughtfully. His grandfather had asked him to try to be friends with Jake this week. "Looks like that's going to be impossible," he mumbled to himself.

Deep in thought, he walked back toward the cabins while Jake took the path toward the lake. Neither saw the bearded man watching them, hidden by the bushes only a few feet from the trail.

Jess slipped quietly out of her bunk and tugged on a pair of jeans. Pulling a sweatshirt over her head, she found her shoes and grabbed the notebook that she called her journal. She headed for a large rock a few yards from the cabin. The grass was wet beneath her feet. The sun was just starting to rise on another day at camp.

She climbed onto the rock and got comfortable. Then she opened her notebook and read what she had written during the first few days at camp. She felt close to God in the woods. Jess began to talk to him. She didn't close her eyes. Instead she watched the early morning sun splinter through the trees and start to dry the dew from the grass. She told God how much she missed her mom and how glad she was that she had found the Ringers after she and her dad had moved to Millersburg. Most of all, she thanked God for loving her and finding her.

After Jess was finished praying, she sat quietly for a few moments before she opened her journal and began to write.

"Jess?" Chris's voice sounded behind her, scattering her thoughts. Hastily Jess closed her journal.

"Hi, Chris . . . ," she stuttered uncertainly. She was glad that Chris couldn't read what she had just been writing because it had been about him!

"You like to get up early, too," Chris commented. Jess nodded as Chris casually joined her on the rock.

32

"What do you think of Jake?" Chris asked abruptly.

"I don't know," Jess answered thoughtfully. "He sure isn't friendly."

"No kidding," Chris said with a trace of sarcasm. "Jim says Pastor Whitehead wants us to be friendly to him. But Jim's already tried and says he's like a grizzly bear."

"He keeps flirting with the older girls, too, like Kate," Jess said. "It makes me not want to go near him."

"We've tried to include him in some stuff this week. Sometimes he's OK, then other times . . ." Chris's voice drifted off. "I think he was in some kind of trouble in the city," he said thoughtfully. "When I mentioned the word *gang,* he almost jumped out of his skin. And this week, some things in our cabin have been disappearing."

"What kind of things?" Jess asked warily, remembering the search through their cabin yesterday for Tina's lost necklace.

"Oh, Willy lost a backpack and Pete lost a camera. We searched our cabin a couple times. Jeff said that the stuff was bound to turn up sooner or later. Then last night, everyone in our cabin except Jake went for a late-night swim. Before we left, I know I put my watch on top of my Bible next to the bed. This morning, it was gone."

Jess looked at Chris. "It does sound like we have a thief at camp."

"Pete's convinced that it's Jake."

Jess watched the sunlight flickering through the trees for a few moments.

Then she said softly, "I remember how tough it was

when I moved to Millersburg. No one really liked me. And I knew your parents made you include me in things."

Chris shifted uncomfortably. What Jess was saying was true. He hadn't really liked her very much at first. It was surprising how much getting to know someone changed things sometimes.

"And you guys were kind of . . . well . . . I was never around anyone who ever talked about Jesus like he was a real person the way you guys did," Jess continued.

"You're right," Chris responded with a tentative smile. "But now . . ."

"Now I know what you mean," Jess said, returning Chris's smile. "Look, Chris, I know Jake's not real nice to anyone. But I want to make sure we give him a chance."

"You may be right," Chris said. He and Jess sat quietly for a few minutes, alone with their thoughts.

Then silently, Jess touched Chris's arm and pointed. There was Jake, slipping out of Cabin 8 with something clenched in his left hand.

"I'm going to follow him," whispered Chris.

"Wait a minute," Jess cautioned, "I think we should tell Jeff."

CHOICE ⇒

If Chris decides to follow Jake, turn to page 8.

If he decides to get Jeff, turn to page 47.

34

Jake followed the path until it forked. He took the left fork. Immediately the forest began to thicken around the path. The light faded until only an occasional shaft of sunlight made its way through the trees.

"This isn't too bad," Jake admitted grudgingly to himself. He had never been alone in the woods before. To the right of the trail, he heard the faint swish of flowing water.

Jake left the path and followed the water's sound deeper into the woods. He walked for a long time. Suddenly the forest fell away, and he was staring down several feet into a rapidly flowing stream. "That must be the stream that feeds into the lake."

He glanced at his watch. "It's getting close to six. I'd better head back." He crashed back through the forest in the direction he thought he had come, but he couldn't find the path. He could still hear the stream's noise faintly behind him.

Breathing heavily, he stood still, unable to decide which way to go.

Suddenly, to the left he heard a faint murmur. The sound came closer. Someone was laughing. Then he heard snatches of conversation:

". . . sure those boys are up to something . . ."

". . . have to get them first . . . ," someone said with a snicker.

"I'm glad we're going canoeing on Wednesday. Maybe we can tip a few canoes."

Jake wasn't sure, but he thought he recognized the voice of Jill, the girl he was sort of attracted to.

"I've never canoed before," someone answered softly.

"No problem, we'll be partners." Jill's voice again.

"But who will Tina canoe with?" the soft voice asked.

"Anyone but that new guy," a different voice responded. "He's really strange. His eyes give me the creeps."

"Why did he come here?"

"Chris says he got in trouble in the city."

"You live next door to his aunt, Jess. What's the story?"

"I'm not really sure. I think his aunt forced him to come to camp. . . ."

The voices faded away. Jake realized with a start that the girls had been talking about him. Stiffly he made his way back through the trees toward the direction of the voices. He found he had been quite close to the path after all. Somehow, he no longer wanted to hike around the lake. It gave him a funny feeling to think that the Ringers didn't like him any more than he liked them. He sighed heavily. *It's going to be a long week.* Slowly he retraced his steps back to the cabin.

By the time Jake got back to the cabin, he had walked for several hours. His legs and feet were sore, and he was craving a cigarette badly. He could hardly wait to get back to his duffel bag and get another pack.

36

He burst through the door, intending to head straight for his bunk. But as he swung it open it caught on something halfway through its swing and stopped abruptly, causing Jake to slam into it full-speed.

"Pghmph! Ouch!" came Steve Barton's voice from the other side of the door. He stepped away from the door, rubbing his knee.

Jake had knocked the side of his head right into the door. "Hey!" he said angrily. He began rubbing his temple and scowled at Steve.

"Hey yourself!" Steve glared back. "That's twice in one day." His tone and face were filled with suspicion. The two stood there, nursing their wounds and not knowing what to say.

"Making a bomb?" Jake joked, noting the screwdriver in Steve's hand. Steve had been kneeling in front of an electrical box in the wall; wires stuck out where an outlet used to be and a minestrone soup of tools and electrical parts were in a toolbox that lay open on the floor at Steve's feet.

Steve didn't reply. Jake just stood there.

Steve glared again. "What are you doing?"

Jake glared back. "What do you mean, 'What am I doing?' I'm getting my stuff."

Steve suddenly realized what was happening. "This is the girl's cabin—Cabin 5."

Jake made a face as if to say, "Freak me out." He looked around. The cabin itself looked exactly like the one he'd left his duffel in, but it wasn't the same. There were more suitcases, for one thing, and Jake could tell from the

things lying around—things that only girls would
bring—that it was definitely a girls' cabin and not a guys'.
"Chill out, buffalo head. I made a mistake."

"No, no. My mistake. I'm sorry. I thought you knew
where you were. These cabins all look the same, I know. It
happens. And I'm not a buffalo head. Your cabin is Cabin
8—over that way, about fifty yards." Steve pointed in the
general direction of the guys' cabin.

Jake only nodded, then turned to go.

"Want to help me? I'm trying to fix this outlet before
dinner. These girls are going to need it for hair dryers,
curling irons, that sort of stuff."

Jake shook his head, then resumed his move out the
door.

"It'll only take a minute."

"No thanks."

Steve threw up his screwdriver in exasperation, and
gave Jake a look to match. Jake froze. "You're going to be
this week's Silverlake Stranger, aren't you?" Steve said with
undisguised disgust.

Jake looked right at Steve. His question had been
thick with disappointment and disgust. More important to
Jake, the "aren't you?" had the sound of destiny, like some
appointment that Jake *had* to make. Jake hated *having* to
do anything, so he decided to find out what Steve meant.
"What's that supposed to mean?" he said roughly.

Steve looked at Jake with obvious frustration. "Every
week somebody comes with an attitude that says, 'I don't
want nothing to do with you.' And they come and do
nothing but keep to themselves all week, saying nothing,

doing nothing, acting like they don't need anybody. Lotta times they don't even use their real names. Completely anonymous. Silverlake Strangers. They come as strangers, get nothing out of being here, and leave as strangers. They know why they're here—to hear about Jesus and what he has to say to them. But instead they just sit in the back row and burp and crack dirty jokes all week, never giving God a chance to speak to them, almost like it's a challenge to prove something. Well, what did God ever do to deserve treatment like that, Jake? All he wants is a hearing from you guys, and then when you have an opportunity—away from all the garbage in the city—you just tune him out. I don't get it, Jake." Steve suddenly stopped talking.

Jake stayed frozen in his place, a million mixed emotions going through him and a million more wild thoughts crowding his head. One second he would think, *This is weird. I can't take this religious fanatic stuff. This is really weird.* And the next second he would think, *I need to listen to this. I need to listen to this.* He didn't know whether to be mad at Steve for lumping him with the "stranger" crowd, or respect the fact that Steve had figured him out.

Did he want to stay and listen, or get mad and leave? He wanted to do both.

If Jake decides to leave, turn to page 106.

If Jake decides to stay, turn to page 5.

Quickly Willy began to back paddle.

"Use your paddle to push off from their canoe, Jake," Willy commanded. Jake pushed hard, and their canoe went sideways in the stream. Willy paddled furiously as the canoe wobbled a few moments in the current and almost spun completely around. Sam and Chris laughed as they kept paddling with the current. From the back of the canoe, Chris halfheartedly splashed Willy as they sped by.

Tina and Jill floated by in their canoe and waved. Just as they were almost past the boys' canoe, Jill turned around and splashed Jake and Willy. The boys could hear her giggle floating back over the water. Jake mumbled something to himself that Willy decided it was probably better he didn't hear. Finally the two boys were able to get their canoe turned around and headed back downstream again.

Up ahead of them, Sam and Chris were in the lead. Jess and Jeff had paused for a few moments in the shallows while Jess put on some extra sunscreen.

"Hey, Jeff," Chris called out as they paddled past, "how much farther to the bridge?"

"About four miles," Jeff called back. "You're the leaders now."

Chris and Sam paddled rapidly downstream. They

had both canoed quite a bit before and had soon caught on to maneuvering the canoe as a team.

"The current's deadly here," Sam said as he noticed the canoe wobbling in the rippling water.

"We can handle it," Chris responded confidently as the canoe steadied once more. "Look!" Chris pointed, "The stream forks up ahead."

"Look! It spoons over there!" replied Sam.

Chris ignored him. "Which way shall we go?" he asked, resting for a moment. "Steve didn't say anything about the stream forking."

"I vote we take the left fork," Sam said. "The right one is for dessert."

"But the current is running faster to the right. It looks like the main part of the river goes that way," Chris suggested. "I think we should go right."

CHOICE ⇉

If Chris and Sam decide to take the right fork, turn to page 80.

If they decide to take the left fork, turn to page 59.

Jake slipped into the alley without being seen.

Now what? he thought. *If I start hitching, someone from the church might see me. I'd better wait until the camp bus leaves before taking off.* Jake noticed the side door to the church basement was slightly ajar.

Perfect, he thought. Opening the basement door, Jake went down the stairs. The church had a unique smell, kind of like pine soap and old books, and it mingled with the smell of cookies that had been brought for that afternoon's vacation Bible school. Jake hadn't eaten breakfast, so he stealthily walked down the hallway toward the cookie aroma.

Several wrapped plates of cookies were sitting on the counter in the kitchen. Jake helped himself to a handful and, still carrying his sleeping bag and duffel, went up a side staircase and into the sanctuary. At the back row of pews, he unrolled his sleeping bag on the floor and settled down to wait until the camp bus had left.

A loud crash of organ music startled Jake so much that he jerked up. He peered over the pew in front of him and saw a white-haired lady sitting at the organ playing furiously. And standing beside her, looking right at Jake, was Pastor Whitehead!

"Oh Jake, I'm so sorry but the camp bus has just left," Pastor Whitehead began, "You must have fallen asleep. . . ."

"What will we do, Leonard?" Mrs. Whitehead had stopped playing and was looking over at Jake, too. "He won't want to miss the whole week of camp!"

"I know!" Pastor Whitehead exclaimed. "The bus is stopping at Fairfax Congregational to pick up another group of campers. That's only a half hour away. If we call that church and tell them to have the bus wait, I can drive Jake there right away."

Jake watched the two earnest faces looking at him. They really seemed to believe that he wanted to go to camp. Shrugging in defeat, he picked up his sleeping bag and duffel and walked out from behind the pews. He thought for a moment about making a break for it, but he knew he wouldn't get very far with all his stuff, and the thought of dodging Bill Grossman all summer still hung like a black cloud over his head.

Sullenly, he turned and went out of the sanctuary.

In a few moments, he and Pastor Whitehead were heading toward Fairfax.

"That car behind us is driving too close," Pastor Whitehead muttered. "I wish people wouldn't do that. It makes me nervous!"

Jake glanced over his shoulder at the car behind them and froze.

Bill Grossman was at the wheel, he was almost sure of it! Jake slid down as far as he could in his seat.

"Are you OK?" Pastor Whitehead asked curiously. "You look frightened. You know, Jake, you don't have to go to camp."

"Yeah, I know," Jake mumbled in reply.

After Pastor Whitehead had made several turns, Jake asked, "Is that car still tailing us?"

Pastor Whitehead glanced in his rearview mirror. "Why, yes, it is still behind us."

Jake felt sick. How could Grossman have possibly known where he was? And to follow him all the way out here? Pastor Whitehead was watching him with some concern.

"Is something bothering you, Jake?" Pastor Whitehead asked. "If there's something you want to talk about, I'm good at keeping secrets." For one wild moment, Jake had the impulse to tell Pastor Whitehead what had happened. But he just shook his head and slid down further in the seat.

Pastor Whitehead turned into the parking lot at Fairfax Congregational. The car behind them slowed for a moment, but then continued down the street.

The yellow bus was waiting for Jake in the parking lot. Pastor Whitehead parked the car and walked with Jake to the bus. A few of the kids were still standing outside the bus door, talking to Jeff. Jake passed them without a word and boarded the bus.

"I hope you have a good time at camp, Jake," Pastor Whitehead called after him.

Then, calling his grandson aside, the pastor quietly spoke a few words to him. Jim listened intently and nodded.

Turn to page 96.

Within minutes, Willy, Jake, and the dark-haired man were squeezed into the front seat of a blue pickup, heading toward the hospital. The man asked Willy a few questions about Jake and what had happened, and Willy answered them.

"You did a good job, son," the man said at last.

Willy stared at the man's profile as he drove. He had high cheekbones and a long straight nose. His hair was tied back with a bandanna.

"What's your name?" Willy asked hesitantly.

"John Silverthorne," the man answered, his eyes never leaving the road.

"Hey, Jake, how are ya doin'?" Willy asked, watching Jake's face turn whiter as the pickup bounced over the ruts in the road.

Jake groaned.

When they got to the hospital, the doctor examined Jake and then took some X rays. "He has quite a knot on his head," the doctor said. "I think someone should check on him several times tonight, just in case. But he'll be fine."

"Cool, thanks ma'am!" Willy exclaimed, as they helped Jake to a chair in the waiting room. "And thanks, Mr. Silverthorne, for all your help."

Just then Steve bounded in with the camp nurse at his side.

"How are you, Jake?" Steve asked.

"He got hit in the head when our canoe flipped over," Willy explained. "But the doctor took some X rays and said he'll be fine."

"I saw your canoe beached by John Silverthorne's place and stopped to check it out. When I couldn't find anyone I called camp and heard you were here, and they stopped by and picked me up on the way," Steve explained.

"Hello, Steve," Mr. Silverthorne said.

Steve turned to where John had been standing in the shadow of the corridor. "John!" he exclaimed. The two men gripped hands. "You certainly have a way of landing on your feet, Willy," Steve said, grinning. "You managed to be rescued by a good friend of mine, John Silverthorne. John's a naturalist in this area. He's doing some important research on the changes that are taking place in the Bluefin River."

"Cool," Willy replied politely.

"John's grandfather was a Cherokee Indian chief," Steve continued with a twinkle in his eye.

"Totally cool!" Willy exclaimed enthusiastically. "Did your grandfather ever tell you any stories?"

"A great many," replied John Silverthorne.

"My great-grandmother Hattie likes to tell stories too," Willy explained proudly.

"Maybe if you've got some time this evening, John, you could come over to camp and tell us one of your grandfather's stories," said Steve.

"I'd be glad to," John responded.

46

Steve and the nurse helped Jake into the camp pickup. Willy rode with Mr. Silverthorne, and by the time they all made it back to Camp Silverlake, a large fire was already blazing. Much to Willy's delight, once Mr. Silverthorne got going, he told story after story about his ancestors and the dilemmas they had to face. Jake, still a little light-headed from his own adventure, sat quietly, taking it all in, thinking of the dilemma *he* would have to face when he got home and wondering, in the face of pressure, what he would choose to do.

CHOICE ⇒

To find out more about Jake and his adventures, turn back to the beginning and make different choices along the way.

Or, turn to page 121.

After a few moments' thought, Chris agreed. Together, he and Jess walked back to Cabin 8. Jess waited a few feet from the door while Chris bounded inside.

"Where's Jeff?" he asked.

"He went to the dining hall," Willy mumbled sleepily, burrowing deeper into his sleeping bag.

"Thanks, Willy." Chris rejoined Jess outside the cabin.

Just then Jake came sauntering up to the cabin. His hands were empty.

"Where were you, Jake?" Chris asked.

"None of your business," Jake responded as he went into the cabin.

As Jess and Chris walked away from the cabin, Pete came out of the woods.

"Hey Pete, you're up early."

"I was following Jake," Pete said, lowering his voice. "I'm sure he's the thief."

"Did you see him take something?" whispered Jess.

Pete hesitated. "Not exactly. But I still think he's been taking the stuff."

Chris looked at Jess. "Let's call a meeting of the Ringers after breakfast in the clearing behind Cabin 8. We can decide what to do then."

48

Turn to page 62.

Willy pushed the door open and walked inside. "Anyone here?" he called. No one answered. He was standing in a small room that looked like the living room. There was a telephone sitting on a table by the window. Willy quietly tiptoed toward the telephone, picked up the receiver, and dialed the operator. Within minutes, he was talking to a camp counselor. He told them what had happened and asked them to send help.

He raced back to the river. When he was almost there, he saw Jake stumbling toward him, supported by a tall, black-haired man.

"Your friend is hurt," the dark-haired man said quietly. "We need to take him to a doctor."

"I know!" exclaimed Willy. "I . . . uh . . . just used your phone. A counselor from Camp Silverlake is coming to pick us up and take us to the hospital."

"Call them back and tell them to meet us there. I'll drive you in now. Your friend needs to see a doctor sooner, not later."

Turn to page 44.

When we were first walking to our cabin," Willy began, "I checked out the girls' cabins and got this idea—"

"Willy's thinking. This could be dangerous!" Pete said with a grin.

"—about a trick we can play on the girls," Willy continued, ignoring the interruption.

"Last year the guys sneaked into one of the girls' cabins and put all the shoes on the roof," Jim volunteered.

"Too tame," scoffed Willy. "I have a rep to maintain."

"My uncle told me about the time the guys hid all the girls' underwear in a tree!" Sam said. Everyone laughed.

"Everyone always steals underwear," Willy said smugly.

"OK, Willy, let's hear it," Jim demanded, "but I have a feeling that we're going to get into trouble. . . ."

Later that night, Cabin 8 was relatively quiet, except for the occasional munching sounds as the Ringers took turns sampling snacks from Willy's goodie bag. Chris was reading, using his flashlight. Sam and Pete were talking quietly. Jake had rolled over against the wall and was probably asleep. Everyone but Jake was waiting.

"Night everyone." Jeff's voice broke the stillness. "I have to go to the dining hall for a short counselor's meeting. Lights out in ten."

"Sure, no problem," Sam could hardly keep the excitement out of his voice. No one said anything as they waited until they were certain that Jeff was out of earshot.

"OK," said Willy, with a twinkle in his eye, "Who's up for a late-night shower?"

The Ringers quietly sneaked out of their cabin and over toward the girls' cabins.

"Where's Jill, Tina, and Jess's cabin?" Jim asked.

"Over there on the right, beside that big tree," Pete answered.

Willy took charge. "Chris, you and Jim stand by the window next to the girls' cabin and listen. When the girls get ready to make one last trip to the bathroom, run as fast as you can to the bridge and tell us. We'll wait."

"Right," Chris whispered. He and Jim sneaked quietly to the girls' cabin. The sounds of singing came from the open window.

Willy, Sam, and Pete scampered to the bridge and jumped into the water as quietly as they could.

"Wow, its cold!"

"And muddy."

They crouched under the bridge, shivering in the dark. Finally they heard the muffled sound of feet running.

"They're coming!" Chris's voice whispered above them.

Willy waited until he heard a girl's giggle. When the girls were almost to the bridge, he nudged Sam.

"Now!" he whispered.

Willy timed it perfectly. Just when he heard the

footsteps crossing the bridge, he reached his hand over the edge of the bridge and grabbed something. An ankle!

Someone screamed. Pete and Sam made snuffling noises and threw some water weeds up in the air over the bridge.

"Help!" screeched Tina. "Something's got my ankle!"

"What is it?" cried Jess.

"A hand!" shrieked Tina as she whirled around and raced back toward the cabin. Jess was right behind her.

"That was great!" Sam said, laughing.

"Perfect!" Willy declared smugly. "The perfect plan."

"Not quite so perfect," Jill's voice came out of the darkness.

Willy jumped a foot. "You scared me!"

"No kidding!" Jill said sarcastically. "Just wait till we get even! Then you'll see the perfect plan!"

THE END

To see if the girls do get them back or to find out what other zany camp antics go on at Silverlake, turn back to the beginning and make different choices along the way.

Or, turn to page 121.

Pushing all thoughts of escape from his mind, Jake reluctantly turned away from the empty alley and got on the bus. He was careful to stuff his duffel bag onto the seat beside him to keep anyone else from sitting there. He might have to go to camp with these kids, but no one said he had to hang out with them. He leaned against the window and closed his eyes.

Back in the parking lot, Willy, Sam, Jim, and Pete were trying to figure out what they would do first when they got to camp. Pete was barely paying attention to the conversation. Out of the corner of his eye he had been watching Jake.

"Who's that kid?" Pete asked Sam suddenly.

"I don't know, but he sure isn't very friendly. I think he's staying with Mrs. Watson, the woman who lives next door to Jessica. When Jess gets here, let's ask her."

"Where's Tina?" asked Jill, as she joined the group, carrying her overnight case and sleeping bag.

Behind Jill, her cousin Chris struggled with two suitcases.

"Why do girls always bring so much stuff?" Chris complained to Willy as he dragged the suitcases toward the bus.

"'Cause they have to look beautiful," groaned Willy, rolling his eyes, and reaching down to grab one of the suitcases to help his friend. "I bet she even has a hair dryer in here."

"No way," retorted Chris, who called out to his cousin, "Hey Jill, are you taking a hair dryer to camp?"

Jill turned around and gave Chris a withering look. "Of course, Chris. Are we going swimming this week, or what?"

"Told ya." Willy grinned and nudged his friend as they reached the bus with the suitcases.

Willy, Sam, Jim, Pete, Chris, Jill, and Tina were "the Ringers," Capitol Community Church's own unofficial gang. They got their name partly from being responsible to ring the bell at church every Sunday morning. The guys always complained that there were girls in the gang, but they didn't really mind. "They can be cool," Willy said once. Besides, Miss Whitehead, their old Sunday school teacher from two years back, was "a girl." And she had called them "ringers" for being so much like Jesus. That was long before the pastor had enlisted their bell-ringing skills. "Remember to be ringers of Jesus," Miss Whitehead would tell them. They didn't always live up to it, but they tried.

"There's Jess!" shouted Jill as Jess and her father pulled up in their blue minivan. Jess was a relatively new friend of the Ringers. Thomas, Jess's dog, was perched in the backseat, looking excitedly at the group.

"Thoma-aa-s, slap me four!" said Sam as Jess piled out of the car and several of the Ringers went over to greet her. "Slip me some claw. Let me see some fur." Thomas licked Sam in the face as Jill and Jess greeted each other.

"I hope you have enough books to last the week," Jess's father teased her as he helped carry her stuff to the bus and kissed her good-bye.

"I'm glad we're going to camp together!" Jill hugged her friend.

"Me too," murmured Jess shyly, smiling at Jill. It hadn't been very long since Jess had moved to Millersburg and had gotten to know the Ringers.

"Look, there's Tina," Jill announced as Tina and her grandmother joined the group.

"Have a wonderful time at camp, girls. I promise to write you each a letter," said Mrs. Whitehead, hugging each girl.

"Everyone's here now," Pastor Whitehead announced, joining his wife. "Time for you to get on the bus. We hope you all have a wonderful week at camp."

"Good-bye!"

"Bye Dad, see you in a week!"

"Bye, Mom!"

Choruses of "Good-bye, Mom and Dad" echoed across the parking lot as the Ringers trooped onto the bus. In the back of the Martins' car, Gracie, the basset hound, howled mournfully. Chris ran over to the car one last time to give Gracie a good-bye hug before he dashed up the bus steps. The door closed behind him and they were on their way!

In the front of the bus, the girls had already started to sing some of their favorite songs.

"Singing," groaned Pete, "Do we have to sing at camp?"

"Absolutely," Jim responded. "And we also have to go swimming and canoeing and horseback riding."

"And we definitely have to raid the girls' cabin," added Willy, pulling out a bag of pretzels from his duffel bag.

"Let's all try to be in the same cabin," Sam declared.

"I'm in Willy's cabin for sure," Chris said with a chuckle, nodding toward Willy's bulging duffel.

"I'm not taking any chances on camp food," Willy explained, patting the duffel full of extra goodies that his mom and grandmother had packed for him.

No one bothered Jake. Jeff Ellers walked up and down the aisle with a clipboard and checked off several times everyone who was there. He managed to stumble only once.

The bus soon left Millersburg. The road climbed quickly toward the Blue Ridge Mountains, and before the Ringers had a chance to be bored, they were there!

The Ringers stepped off the bus. The first person they saw was a muscular, blond-haired man in a camp T-shirt with a clipboard in one hand and a whistle around his neck.

"Welcome to Camp Silverlake. I'm Steve Barton, the activities director," he greeted them warmly.

"Wow, he's big," whispered Jill.

Jeff Ellers stepped forward and shook Steve's hand.

"We're sure glad to be here, Steve," Jeff said excitedly, pumping Steve's hand as he was handed a list of names.

"And we're glad to have you." Steve smiled at Jeff and turned to address the group. "The staff at Camp Silverlake is glad that all of you are here and wants you to enjoy your week. This week, you will be part of a team with your cabin mates. Learn to stick together and look out for each other."

Pete wondered if it was his imagination or if Steve had really looked at Jake for an extra moment before he continued. "Your cabin mates will be your responsibility and you will be theirs as well. We're going to be doing some pretty exciting things this week. You'll need to work together with your group. Pay attention while I read off your names and your cabin numbers."

Steve paused a moment, looked at his clipboard, and began to read off names. When he got to Cabin 5, Jill, Tina, and Jessica's names were all called.

When he had finished, he said, "OK, follow your counselors to your cabins. After you get settled in, I want Cabins 6 through 8 to meet me at the lake for our camp swim test. Any questions?"

Each Ringer's hand went up.

"You forgot us!" exclaimed Sam.

Glancing down at his clipboard, Steve said, "Oops! Sorry about that. OK, you guys and Jake are all together in Cabin 8."

"Who's our counselor?" asked Pete.

"I am," Jeff responded happily, waving the list Steve had given him. "I knew you guys all wanted to be together so I made sure we could all bunk in the same cabin."

"Great!" Sam exclaimed.

"Yeah, great," Jake echoed softly as he deliberately trailed several feet behind the other guys as they followed Jeff to their cabin.

58

"Here we are," Jeff proclaimed. "This week you'll be the Ringers of Cabin 8."

"Awesome!" exclaimed Chris. "I can't wait to go swimming. That bus sure was hot."

Quickly everyone threw their sleeping bags and suitcases onto the bunks and changed into their swimming trunks. Jake picked the bunk that was the farthest away from the door. No one offered to bunk with him.

"Race you to the lake, Sam!" shouted Willy, as he sprinted out the cabin door. Sam raced after Willy down the path to the lake. The rest of the Ringers followed. Jake walked as slowly as he possibly could behind the group.

"Hey Jeff, do you think we can go canoeing on the lake after supper?" Chris asked, as he and Pete joined their counselor on the path.

"Don't see why not," Jeff responded.

"I remember the all-day canoe trip last year," Jim began. "Are we going to go again this year?"

At that moment, Chris spotted Tina, Jill, and Jess walking through the trees.

"Hey, girls!" he called out, "Where are you going?"

"To show Jess the lake!" Tina called back.

"That's where we're headed," Chris said. "Come on!"

Turn to page 87.

I still vote for left. How 'bout it, Kimosabe?" Sam suggested.

"OK, Sam, we'll go left," agreed Chris, switching his paddle to the right side of the canoe and taking a few deep strokes. The canoe slipped into the wide left fork and immediately slowed down.

"The current's not very swift here," Chris commented. Sam said nothing.

The day was warm. Both boys decided to pull over into the shallows and take off their shirts. The water continued to move more slowly, until the canoe was drifting lazily along.

"Hey, Chris," Sam exclaimed, "Take a look at the water. It's really clear."

Chris looked over the side of the canoe. He could see schools of small minnows swimming by. "Yeah, but it's getting shallower," he commented.

Before long, the stream was less than a foot deep. The bottom of the canoe began to scrape over rocks.

"I think we'll have to get out, Sam," Chris said, starting to untie his shoes.

Slowly the canoe scraped to a stop. Sam looked over the side. "I guess you're right," he replied as he began taking off his shoes and socks.

Both boys stepped out of the canoe. Without their

weight, the canoe floated a little longer as they walked beside it. Then the stream narrowed further until it was little more than a trickle.

"The stream—she be squirt-gun-sized," said Sam. "Now what?"

"We'll have to carry the canoe, I guess," Chris responded.

They dragged the canoe out of the water. Both boys put on their shoes and socks and picked up the canoe, balancing it over their heads. It was a great deal heavier than they had thought it would be. The weight gave Sam second thoughts about continuing on.

"Tell you what, Sam," Chris said, "let's put the canoe down and walk to the right, straight through the woods, and see if we can't hear the other stream. If we don't, then we retrace our steps and get back in the canoe and paddle back to the fork in the stream."

Sam agreed. The boys lowered the canoe from their shoulders and walked through the woods. In a very short time, they heard the sounds of the other stream.

They were jogging back to their beached canoe when Sam suddenly clutched Chris's arm.

"What's that?" he whispered.

"What?" Chris questioned. Sam pointed to an especially thick group of trees on the right. "I don't see anything."

"I thought I saw somebody."

Chris knew Sam too well to take him seriously. He shrugged. "It's probably just a crazed killer who escaped from prison. Come on, let's get the canoe."

"No, this time I'm *serious,*" Sam protested.

Chris laughed. "Yeah, right. Come on, Tonto."

Sam followed, but he kept glancing behind him just in case. They reached their beached canoe and lifted it over their heads. As they walked back to the stream, he said, "Someone's watching us, Chris. I can feel their eyes on my back."

"You've seen too many horror movies," Chris scoffed.

"Maybe," Sam agreed uneasily, "but let's get out of here."

When they finally reached the bank, they realized that there was an eight-foot drop to the stream!

"Now what?" Chris exclaimed.

"Well," said Sam reflectively, "if we both lean over the bank on our stomachs, we can lower the canoe into the water."

"Then how do we get in it?" asked Chris, puzzled.

"We'll have to run downstream, scramble down the bank, and swim to the canoe as it floats past."

Chris disagreed. "I think we should keep walking with the canoe downstream. Maybe the bank won't be so steep and there could be a place to put the canoe in up ahead."

CHOICE

If the boys decide to drop the canoe into the stream and try to scramble in, turn to page 101.

If they decide to keep walking downstream, turn to page 83.

62

After breakfast, all the Ringers gathered in the clearing as Chris suggested.

"Several things have been missing this week," Chris began.

"My camera," Pete interrupted.

"My backpack," said Willy.

"Yeah, and Tina's necklace and my watch," Chris continued. "Does anybody have any ideas about who it might be?"

"I think it's Jake," Pete stated. Several of the other Ringers nodded.

"Innocent until proven guilty," Jim said. "We need some evidence before we accuse the guy of stealing."

"We need a plan," Willy said, "to catch the thief."

"What kind of plan?" asked Tina.

"How about a trap?" Sam said. "We'll put something out that the thief will want and then we'll hide and watch to see if he takes it."

"What about mealtimes?" asked Pete.

"That's when he'd most likely show up," said Willy, "'cause he'd know no one was around."

"Sounds like a good plan," Jim agreed. "Let's bait the trap by putting something out on the picnic table by our cabin, and we'll take turns hanging out in the cabin until the thief comes."

"OK by me," said Sam.

Chris pulled out a notebook. "I'm making a list of times. Everyone pick a time and sign up."

"We need to sign up in pairs," Jill advised, "so one person can go get the others while one person follows the thief."

"Let's do it!" Willy said enthusiastically.

The Ringers went to their morning activities, all except Sam and Pete, who had the first shift. On their way into the cabin, they laid Jim's silver-plated compass and new binoculars on the picnic table.

By dinnertime, the thief still had not made an appearance. It was Chris and Jim's turn to watch.

"Jim, can I talk to you a minute?" Jeff called as the two boys were hurrying to take their place in the cabin.

"Go on ahead," Jim whispered to Chris, "I'll meet you later."

Chris hurried to the cabin and took Tina and Jill's place while Jim joined Jeff heading to the dining room. As he looked out the window, he saw Jake coming out of the woods. Chris held his breath as Jake walked to the picnic table and picked up the compass and binoculars!

"He is the thief," Chris breathed to himself.

Jake opened the door of the cabin and halted when he saw Chris's angry face.

"What's with you?" he questioned as he tossed the things on Jim's bed.

"What were you doing with Jim's gear?" Chris accused.

"It was outside on the picnic table, dork. Someone might have stolen it. Or it could've got rained on. Relax,"

Jake sneered, suddenly understanding Chris's anger. "If I was gonna steal something, it wouldn't be a lousy compass."

"That stuff was bait to catch the thief," Chris stated, his eyes never leaving Jake's face.

Jake stared at Chris, ready for any sudden move that Chris might make. The dinner bell rang loudly. Both boys could hear everyone heading to the mess hall, but neither moved.

Suddenly, Jake's eyes flickered toward the window. Silently he motioned for Chris to look.

Chris glanced at the window. Then his eyes widened as he stared at a thin, bearded man going into Cabin 4!

"He looks like that Nate Sares guy I ran into in the woods," whispered Jake. "And he's still carrying that tackle box."

They waited. In a few moments, the man slipped out of the cabin. He was still carrying the tackle box as well as two cameras and a small suitcase. He paused at the cabin door and looked around before he headed for the path behind the woods.

Silently, Jake turned and headed for the cabin door. "I'll follow him," he hissed. "You go get the others and follow the trail I mark."

Chris couldn't seem to move. Nothing was happening the way he had expected.

"Go!" Jake prodded as he soundlessly slipped out the door.

Chris followed, then started to sprint toward the mess hall. He paused and looked over his shoulder for a moment. He couldn't see either Jake or the thief amongst the trees.

I should follow them, he thought. *What if that man knows Jake's following him and tries to attack him? But someone needs to sound the alarm. What should I do?*

CHOICE

If Chris decides to go after Jake, turn to page 15.

If he decides to go get the others, turn to page 115.

Recognizing the danger, Jim simply decided to overrule Willy. "Well, I'm going," he said, and took a deep breath and began to swim for the shore. Willy tried to protest, but it was no use.

The wind was blowing fiercely now, whipping the lake into small waves. Jim could barely see the shore. He swam steadily for several minutes in the direction of the camp before he began to get tired. Remembering what Jeff had taught them, he rolled onto his back and floated while he caught his breath, rain falling softly around him.

Suddenly a streak of lightning blazed across the sky. Moments later, thunder rumbled.

Jim prayed, "Please, dear God, take care of Pete and Willy and please help me to make it to shore quickly."

Jim flipped back onto his stomach and began to swim again. He tried not to think about how exhausted he was or about the storm breaking behind him. Instead he focused on putting one arm in front of the other. He kept swimming.

When he stopped for a moment to catch his breath, he heard another sound besides the thunder. It was the steady drone of a motor.

Suddenly, from around the other side of the island, Jim saw a small motorboat churning toward him. He waved his arms wildly when he spotted Steve's blond hair above the wheel. In a few moments, he was sitting beside Steve in the front of the boat, wrapped in towels.

"Willy and Pete are still with the sailboat," he gasped when he could get his breath.

"Which way?" Steve asked urgently.

Jim pointed in the direction from which he had come. Soon the small motorboat rounded the island.

"There's the sailboat!" cried Jim, pointing to the yellow-and-white sail floating in the water. Steve headed straight toward it.

"Do you see Willy and Pete?" asked Steve. The sailboat was floating in the water near the spot where Jim had left it, but Willy and Pete were nowhere in sight.

Jim swallowed hard and tried not to panic. "They were here just fifteen minutes ago," he stammered, his teeth chattering.

Steve cut the motor and stripped off his shirt. "Start calling their names and keep watching for them," he commanded. "I'm going to dive a few times around the sailboat."

"Willy! Pete!" Jim shouted over and over. No one answered. He peered through the rain for any sign of his friends. He couldn't see them anywhere.

Several minutes later Steve climbed back into the motorboat. "They're not under the boat," he said, starting the motor. "I'm going to take you back to camp and organize a search party."

"What about the boat?"

"Jim, we're going to have to leave it. It's too dangerous with this lightning to try to take it in. We've got to find Pete and Willy first." Steve paused and said quietly, "The boat'll be fine, I just hope Willy and Pete are."

Jim closed his eyes. He didn't even try to stop the tears that were gliding down his cheeks and mingling with the rain. "Oh, Lord," he prayed, "please don't let anything happen to Pete and Willy." He felt the strong clasp of Steve's hand on his shoulder.

The motorboat accelerated rapidly, skimming over the water. Jim opened his eyes and watched the dock of Camp Silverlake come closer. When the motorboat was almost to the dock, the deep chime of the camp bell boomed out over the water.

"That could be good news, Jim," Steve said as he docked the motorboat and bounded onto the dock. Jim was right beside him. Together they raced to the dining hall.

When they reached the brightly lit dining hall, Pete and Willy were sitting by a table close to the fireplace, surrounded by Jeff and Heather and the other Ringers.

"Jim!" Pete cried, "you made it!"

"Yeah, Steve picked me up in the motorboat. Boy, am I glad to see you guys!" Jim exclaimed, high-fiving his friends. "How'd you guys get back?"

"A couple of fisherman were rowing to their cabin and spotted our sailboat," Willy explained. "They pulled us into their boat. When we got back to their cabin, we used their phone and called Jeff."

"That was quite an adventure you guys had," Jeff

responded. "I, for one, am glad you all stayed calm and got back safely."

Jim closed his eyes and whispered, "Thank you, Lord Jesus," before rejoining the conversation with his friends.

THE END

Turn to page 120.

The morning of the canoe trip was cloudy.

"It looks like it can't decide if it's going to rain or not," Jeff commented, looking up at the sky.

"Be sure to put on plenty of sunscreen," cautioned Heather Roberts, the counselor for Cabin 5. "You can still get a bad burn on days like this, especially when you spend time on the water."

Steve was waiting for everyone by the dining hall with his ever-present clipboard in his hand. "All right, campers, here's what you've been waiting for: the all-day canoe trip," he announced enthusiastically.

"How can anyone be so cheerful this early in the morning?" moaned Tina.

"Today, we're going to canoe the Bluefin River," Steve continued. "That's the river that feeds into Silver Lake. The camp bus will take us about fifteen miles upstream. This morning, we'll canoe about nine miles, leaving an easy float for after lunch. We'll make it back to Camp Silverlake about dinnertime and have a cookout by the lake. We'll assign you partners for the first leg of the trip. Then we'll switch everyone around after lunch. Everybody ready?"

A cheer went up from Cabin 8. Tina groaned again.

"OK, let's go," Steve declared.

The Ringers from Cabin 8 bounded onto the bus. The girls followed a little more slowly. As the bus started to pull out of the camp parking lot, Jeff pulled a list out of his pocket and began to read off the names of canoeing partners.

"Sam and Chris, Jim and Pete, Tina and Jill, Jeff and Jess—" Jeff looked up to grin at Jess—"Jake and Willy."

Willy tried not to show his disappointment about having Jake as a partner. *At least it's only half the trip,* he thought to himself.

When the bus finally arrived at the drop-off point, Steve started to pass out life preservers.

"The current is pretty slow today," Steve explained, "but be on the lookout for submerged trees or underwater rocks, as well as places where the current speeds up and slows down. Those places can be tricky. And be sure to wear your life preservers at all times, no matter how good a swimmer you are! The river isn't very deep, but we want to be careful."

"Right," Jeff agreed, strapping on his life vest. "We'll stop for lunch at the first bridge. Whoever gets there first, pull your canoe out of the water and wait for the others. OK, Jess, let's go!" Jess and Jeff were the first to get their canoe into the water. Jess sat in the front of the canoe as Jeff pushed off.

"Hey, Jake," Willy asked casually as he gathered two paddles from the pile on the shore, "have you ever canoed before?"

Jake wouldn't answer. He just shrugged.

"OK," Willy said with a sigh, "why don't you get in the front of the canoe and I'll steer."

Jake and Willy paddled slowly away from the bank. Willy was surprised to see that Jake paddled at all.

"The guy in front is the lookout," Willy explained. "He's the one who tells the guy in back if there's a submerged rock or log or rapids or anything like that."

"Where'd you get to be such a canoe expert?" sneered Jake.

"My dad and I used to go canoeing a lot in the summer when we lived in Missouri," Willy explained. "We canoed on the Black River and the Current River. What I liked the most was—"

"OK," Jake interrupted. "I get the picture."

Willy stopped talking, and Jake didn't volunteer any conversation. For the next hour, the boys canoed in silence.

Finally Jake spoke. "Snake," he said dryly.

"Wh-What?" stuttered Willy.

"To your left. A snake."

Willy stared at the dark body that slithered past, its head barely visible above the current.

"Yuch," Willy said with a shiver. "Those things give me the creeps."

"Yeah," Jake responded, thinking of the Vipers. "Just stay out of their way and they won't bite you."

The canoe rounded the bend. Willy saw a water fight happening between Sam and Chris and Tina and Jill.

Jake ignored both canoes as theirs glided past. Willy smiled when he saw how reluctant everyone was to splash Jake. That could be a definite advantage. Willy also noticed that Jake was beginning to handle his paddle more easily.

"Hey, Jake," Willy called out softly when they were

out of earshot of the splashing canoes, "let's pull over into the weeds by the side of the stream. When Chris and Sam come past, let's splash 'em!"

Jake merely grunted in reply, but he helped Willy paddle the canoe into the shallow water by the bank of the river. Their canoe was almost concealed by the low branches of the trees growing close to the stream. Just as Chris and Sam rounded the bend, Willy shot the canoe forward.

"Oh no!" he exclaimed. Too late, he realized that he had steered their canoe too sharply across the current. In a few seconds, their canoe would crash into the side of Chris and Sam's canoe. Willy tried frantically to turn their canoe quickly enough to bring it alongside Chris and Sam's canoe, but they were shooting forward too rapidly. "We're going to crash!" Willy yelled.

"Back paddle!" shouted Chris, desperately trying to maneuver out of the way of Willy and Jake's canoe.

CHOICE ⟹

If the canoes crash together, turn to page 103.

If everyone decides to back paddle and forget about splashing each other, turn to page 39.

For a fleeting moment, Jake thought about rejoining the Ringers. But he soon shook himself out of it. He didn't want to even *be* at camp in the first place. And if he had any choice in the matter, he would stay as far away from the Ringers as possible.

Turn to page 29.

The boathouse was abandoned.

"Are you sure it's OK to take a sailboat?" Jim questioned.

"Sure," Willy reassured him, "I left Jeff a note and told him we were going to go sailing during free time."

"Looks cloudy to me," Pete commented, looking up at the sky.

"The wind will be great for sailing," Willy declared with a smile as he began to push the boat off the shore. "OK, I'll steer. Jim, you tighten the sheet. When we are deep enough, Pete, remember to put in the dagger board."

Willy jumped onto the back of the boat. Jim was trying to manage the sail. He struggled for a few moments until suddenly the wind caught the sail perfectly. The white canvas billowed out and grew taut.

"Trim the sail," instructed Willy, doing his best to imitate Steve.

"Like this?" questioned Jim as he tightened the sheet.

"Exactly," Willy replied as the sailboat tilted gently to one side. The fabric of the sail grew taut as the wind carried the boat along.

"Where to, guys?" shouted Willy over the noise of the wind and the spray.

"Why don't we explore the far side of the lake?" suggested Pete, pointing to a spot beyond the small island that jutted up from the middle of the lake.

"Sounds good to me!" exclaimed Willy as he angled the sailboat to the right of the island. The wind picked up. In no time at all the boat was skimming over the water, flying past the small island. Behind the island, the shoreline of Camp Silverlake disappeared from view.

"Wow, this is neat!" Pete exclaimed as he leaned over the side of the boat to catch the spray. Just as he straightened up, the wind gusted unexpectedly from a different direction. The boon of the sail swung around and caught Pete across the shoulder and neck, pushing him off balance. It happened so fast that he didn't even have a chance to grab anything before he fell overboard.

"Let go of the rope, Jim!" cried Willy. Jim immediately let go of the sheet. The sailboat wobbled a few minutes and then stopped in the water.

Pete was bobbing in the water a few yards behind the sailboat, dazed from the blow. "Come on, Pete, swim! You're only a few yards from the boat!" exclaimed Jim. Pete kicked as hard as he could and finally reached the side of the boat. Jim leaned over to grab his arms, and Willy dropped the rudder to help.

The weight of all three boys on one side of the craft was too much for the little sailboat. It faltered a minute and then tipped gracefully over onto its side in the water, dumping the boys with it.

"Now what?" sputtered Willy as he bobbed to the surface. Jim helped free Pete from the tangled sail. Together they swam around to the other side of the sailboat.

"If we all three push down hard on the dagger board, I think we can flip the boat up again," Jim said.

Two tries later, the boys were out of breath.

"Wow, this water's really cold, " Pete said, shivering.

"It's the wind," said Jim uneasily, looking up at the darkening sky. "I think a storm's coming."

"We shouldn't be in the water if there's lightning," Willy added. "Maybe we should try to swim for shore."

"I don't think I can make it," Pete said hesitantly. "I don't feel too good. Why don't you guys go ahead and send back some help? I can just float here with the boat."

But Willy insisted, "No, we all stay together. C'mon, guys, if we just push hard on the dagger board one more time, we can get this boat upright."

Giving it one more shot, the three boys pushed down with all their might. The sailboat wobbled for a moment, then sank back into the water.

"It's no use," Pete declared. "I'll be OK staying with the boat. Go ahead, Jim, you're the best swimmer. Why don't you swim for shore and bring back help?"

"Look!" said Willy, pointing to the right of them. The sky was rapidly growing dark. A sheet of rain came gliding over the water. "At least we're already wet!" Willy joked.

"I'll go get some help," said Jim.

"No, we've got to stay with the boat!" Willy insisted stubbornly.

CHOICE ⇒

If Jim stays with the boat, turn to page 24.

If he tries to swim and get help, turn to page 66.

Let it go, Chris," Willy finally said. "We'll have a better time without him anyway."

Chris glared at Jake's back as he disappeared into the forest.

"OK," he said reluctantly. "But I don't like anybody bad-mouthing my friends."

"I vote we get in this canoe," Sam said, shivering. "Unless maybe you guys would rather walk, too?"

Chris snorted. "Fat chance."

The three friends took turns steadying the canoe while they all got in.

"This is cool with three," Willy observed, sitting in the middle of the canoe watching Sam and Chris paddle.

"You'll get your turn, Willy," Sam promised as they headed toward the bridge.

"Hey, look, there's Jill and Tina up ahead. It looks like they've got your canoe, Willy." They noticed an empty canoe tied to the back of the girls' canoe.

"Great!" Willy exclaimed, "Now all we have to worry about is this dent. . . ."

"What's with the *we?*" Sam teased.

When they finally got to the bridge for lunch, Jake was nowhere to be seen.

"What happened to Jake, Willy?" Jeff asked when he saw the empty canoe.

The three Ringers took turns telling the story. Jeff took the camp truck to hunt for Jake and missed the rest of the canoe trip.

Later that night Jake returned, but he wouldn't tell anyone where he'd been. Steve almost decided to send him home but relented and gave him one more chance, but Jake had to forfeit his free time for the rest of the week.

After they heard what had happened, all the Ringers avoided Jake, except for Jess, who felt sorry for him and tried several times to start up conversations. But Jake never answered her questions, so after a while she gave up, too. After the week of camp was over, Jake went back to the city, and the Ringers didn't see him again that summer.

THE END

Turn to page 121.

To find out what might have happened to Jake, turn to page 70 and make different choices along the way.

If you insist, Kimosabe," Sam agreed, and Chris steered toward the swifter current.

Within a few minutes Chris shouted, "I see the bridge up ahead!"

"Great!" Sam exclaimed, "I'm starved!"

When they reached the bridge, the boys pulled their canoe out onto the beach underneath the bridge.

Two of the camp staffers were waiting for them. Together, they helped unload the lunch from the camp's pickup truck. One by one the other canoers straggled in.

Steve was the last one to join the group.

Before they dug into their meal, Jeff thanked God for the food and for giving everyone safety.

"You made good time!" Jeff said approvingly, as they were finishing their ice-cream sandwiches. "Now it's time for the afternoon partner assignments. I'll take Pete with me; Jill, you go with Jess; Tina, you'll be with Jim; Willy, you and—"

"I'd like to stay with Jake," Willy spoke up, surprising everyone—especially Jake.

"OK, Willy," Jeff said after a pause. "Then I guess Chris and Sam will canoe together again. That OK with you guys?" Chris and Sam both nodded.

"Sounds good to me, too." Willy beamed.

"I have a few more water-fight plans," Willy said to

Jake, lowering his voice so that only Jake could hear, "and together, you and I can take on Chris and Sam." Jake said nothing.

"Before we start canoeing again, how about a swim?" Jim asked. Steve nodded. Several of the guys pulled off their shirts and splashed into the water.

"What's the matter, Jill? Don't you want to mess up your hair?" Sam teased when none of the girls made a move to get into the water.

"No thanks," Jill said with a shudder. "Tina and I saw a snake this morning. I really don't want to swim with snakes."

Jake watched everyone swimming and wished that he could swim. He didn't want to look stupid and just wade into the water, so he sat on the bank and tried to look like he didn't care.

"C'mon in, Jake," Willy spoke encouragingly. "It's a great way to cool off!"

Jake heard Steve's voice behind him. "I'll be right beside you, Jake," he said quietly. "Let's go in."

Reluctantly, Jake pulled off his shirt and eased into the water. Steve noticed a thin white scar running under Jake's arm across his chest. Willy and Chris saw the scar, too, but nobody had the nerve to ask how he got it.

Soon the Ringers were cooled off and ready to travel. Everyone got into their canoes and pushed off. Willy and Jake ambushed Chris and Sam and splashed them hard.

"That was great," declared Willy with a laugh as he and Jake canoed downstream. "We really got them good!

But we'll have to watch out 'cause they'll try to get us back for sure!"

"Hey," Jake said, "there's a tree under the water in front of us."

"Which way do I steer?" asked Willy, all traces of laughter gone.

"Go left," Jake said uncertainly.

Willy guided the canoe to the left. As they passed the tree, he leaned over to have a better look. At that moment, the current eddied swiftly around the tree. The canoe tipped sharply to one side and overturned. Willy and Jake plunged into the water, soaking themselves and capsizing the canoe.

"Whew! That's one way to get cool, right, Jake?" sputtered Willy as he surfaced beside the canoe. "At least I was able to grab the canoe . . . Jake?" he called uncertainly, looking around.

"Jake?" he called again.

Suddenly he looked downstream and saw Jake wearing his orange life vest, bobbing down the stream. Jake didn't look like he was moving.

"Jake!" Willy called louder. *Oh no, what should I do?* he thought to himself.

CHOICE ⇒

If Willy tries to swim after Jake, turn to page 26.

If he tries to turn the canoe over and use it to rescue Jake, turn to page 108.

Well, let's go downstream, then," said Sam. "I'm always looking for opportunities to lift weights."

The boys hoisted the canoe back onto their shoulders and continued downstream. The day was getting hotter and hotter. Chris could feel the sweat trickling down the back of his neck.

"Walking under this canoe is like being in a tin can!" Sam complained.

"Look," Chris called out, "I can see a bridge up ahead!"

"Yeah, and this path is going downhill!"

"Yeah!" Chris exclaimed, picking up the pace. "Let's put the canoe in the river now!"

Behind Chris, Sam suddenly stumbled over a tree root, and fell to the side of the path. The canoe clattered to the ground.

"Urghh!" Sam groaned, grabbing his ankle.

Chris turned around to help, one of the paddles still in his hand. Suddenly, he froze. "Don't move, Sam!" he said in a panic. "Snake!"

Sam stopped in the middle of getting up, forgetting the throbbing in his ankle. "Where?"

Chris pointed silently toward the brightly patterned serpent curving across the trail in front of him. It slithered slowly toward Sam.

"Don't move!" Chris breathed.

Sam stared at the hourglass pattern on the snake's back. The snake's tongue darted menacingly in and out of its broad, blunt, triangular head. The snake rustled a few feet from Sam's outstretched leg and then stopped. "Chris," Sam said, trying to control his fear.

Chris moved quietly over to Sam, trying to sneak up on the snake. He slowly raised his paddle as Sam watched the snake watching him. "Oh God, please don't let him miss," Sam prayed automatically.

Chris brought the paddle down hard. Sam leaped up and jumped back, his eyes fixed on Chris's target. With his landing he froze again and looked. The snake's head lay crushed beneath Chris's paddle.

"Bullseye!" Sam squeaked. "Torpedo right to the engine room! Oh, thank you, Lord Jesus!"

Chris let out a huge sigh, then poked his victim to make sure it was dead. It was. After some debate about who would carry their "prize kill," they put it in the canoe, which they dragged to the bank and back into the water. "That was a close one!" Chris let out his breath when they were both safely in the canoe.

"Too close for comfort!" Sam replied. They paddled furiously toward the bridge. The rest of the Ringers were already waiting at the bank by the bridge.

"Boy, it took you guys long enough to get here!" Willy teased. "We saw you guys walking with the canoe. Get tired of paddling?"

"Not funny, Willster," Sam remarked, pulling their canoe onto the beach.

"Guess it shows who the best canoers are, right, Jake?"

Startled to be mentioned, Jake glanced up and nodded.

"We saw a snake!" Sam exclaimed.

"So did we," Willy bragged. "No big deal."

"This one slithered right next to Sam," Chris added.

"*Still* no big deal," Willy scoffed.

"What'd the snake look like?" Steve asked, coming over to join the group.

"It had an ugly nose and diamond-shaped-thingies on its back," Chris said, "like this—" He reached into the canoe and held up the snake.

"Whoa!" everyone said at once.

"A copperhead," Steve said matter-of-factly.

"A Duracell snake! Awesome!" Sam exclaimed.

Jake sneered. "More like a deadly one. Good thing you killed it."

"*Deadly?*" Sam said nervously.

Steve nodded. "One of the deadliest in North America."

Sam walked over to the snake and shook his finger at it. "*Bad* snake."

"A deadly snake, but it's still one of God's creatures," Jim said. "There are a ton of those kind of animals in Brazil's rain forest. When you're around them as much as Tina and I were, you learn to respect them—and God. It's amazing what some of them can do."

With that, the pump was primed for more stories about danger. Jim and Tina told a few about Brazil. Willy told a few that his great-grandmother Hattie had told him about slaves trying to escape. And Jake, loosening up a bit, showed them a scar he'd gotten from rough living in the city and alluded to his mix-up with the Vipers. It made them all realize once again just how much God watched over them day after day.

Something they would come to appreciate even more as the week wore on at Camp Silverlake.

THE END

To find out more about the dangers Jake and the Ringers face at Silverlake, go back to the beginning and make different choices along the way.

Turn to page 121.

Tina, Jill, and Jess joined the boys.

"Boy, our counselor is so cool," Jill began. "Her name is Heather Roberts and she has her own horse. She promised to take us riding on Thursday during free time."

"Guess who else is in our cabin, Jim?" Tina teased her brother. "Rebecca Thomas. Remember her from last year?"

"Why Jim, you're blushing!" Jess said with surprise. Jill laughed.

Hearing the girls talk about who was in their cabin reminded Pete of Jake. Pete glanced back at the path to see if he was still following the group. He turned around just in time to see Jake slipping quietly into the woods.

Good riddance, Pete thought. *That is one strange kid.* Then he remembered Steve's talk when they had arrived at camp: "This week, you will be part of a team with your cabin mates. Learn to stick together and look out for each other."

Right, Pete thought as they hiked down the path to the lake. *That's one kid who can look out for himself!*

"Wow, I can see why they call this place Camp Silverlake!" Chris exclaimed as the Ringers paused by the lakeshore to watch the late-afternoon sun sparkle over the water.

"It really is beautiful," Jess said with a sigh.

"Let's go check out the horses now," Jill urged them, clearly getting impatient.

"OK by me," Tina agreed, then added, "Why don't we all meet in the dining hall and sit together at dinner?"

The boys agreed. "First one in the dining hall, save a table for the Ringers," Jim called as the girls hiked back up the hill toward the stables.

On the dock by the lake, Steve was waiting. Jeff ambled over to him. They talked for a few minutes, but the Ringers couldn't hear what they said.

"OK, boys," Steve began after he joined the group on the shore. "What are some of the rules for safe swimming?"

"Never swim alone."

"Never dive unless you know how deep the water is."

"Right." Steve continued, "What should you do if you see someone in trouble in the water?"

"First take a towel or a tree branch and have them try to grab on to those things. Only go in yourself as a last resort," Chris answered immediately.

"Excellent," Steve replied. "I guess Jeff's been teaching you about water safety."

The Ringers looked puzzled. They didn't think of the bean pole Jeff as being capable of teaching any physical skill.

Steve smiled at their confusion. "Guys, I'm going to let you in on a little secret: Jeff Ellers is a great swimmer. He and I used to swim on the same team in college, and he always beat me."

The Ringers really liked Jeff, but as they looked from Steve's muscled chest to the skinny shoulders of their youth group leader, they wondered if Steve was making some kind of joke at Jeff's expense.

Steve grinned. "Go ahead, Jeff, why don't you take the swimming test first and show them how it's done?"

"Sure." Jeff nodded, smiling. "How about holding my glasses, Chris?" After giving his glasses to Chris, Jeff walked to the end of the dock and jumped in. His head bobbed for a moment under the water, then he quickly pulled himself up onto the dock.

"Before you dive, always check to see how deep the water is," Jeff reminded them. Then he dove cleanly into the lake and swam rapidly out to the raft that was floating about fifty yards from the lake's shore. Jeff swiftly turned underwater, and raced back to the dock.

"Wow, he's really fast!" exclaimed Sam.

"Hey, Jeff, we didn't know you could swim like that!"

Jeff smiled as he pulled himself out of the water and put his glasses back on. Steve handed him the clipboard.

"I think you can take it from here, Jeff," Steve said. "I'll see all of you at supper." He started to hike up the hill toward the camp.

"OK, Cabin 8," Jeff called, "who wants to go first?"

Chris, Willy, and Jim splashed into the water together and raced each other to the raft and back to shore.

"Nice job, guys," Jeff said approvingly. The boys formed groups of twos and threes and took turns swimming out to the raft.

"OK, Sam, it's your turn," Jeff said as he watched the remaining swimmers getting out of the water.

Sam looked at the raft and felt a familiar fear clutch at

his stomach. He was terrified that he couldn't make it to the raft and back. "What happens if I don't take the test, Jeff?" he asked weakly.

"You won't be able to go in the lake during free swim," Jeff responded. When Sam hesitated, Jeff added, "Let me watch you swim here in the roped-off area. It isn't over your head."

Sam got into the water and swam confidently in the chest-deep water. He knew his feet could touch the bottom. After he swam back and forth, Jeff said thoughtfully, "You're not a bad swimmer, Sam. You shouldn't have any problem swimming to the raft and back. If you feel frightened, remember to turn over on your back and float for a minute to catch your breath. C'mon, I'll swim alongside you."

Jeff placed Steve's clipboard on the dock, took off his glasses, and laid them on top. He jumped into the water beside Sam.

Sam heard the Ringers on the shore offering encouragement. He looked out at the bobbing raft. It was so far away. If only the water wasn't over his head, he thought, then he wouldn't be so frightened. He really didn't want to give up free swims with the guys, but he didn't think he could make it to the raft and back without panicking.

"C'mon dude, you can do it!" Willy called impatiently from the shore. "Get it over with so we can take over this place!"

Jeff waited quietly beside Sam.

CHOICE

If Sam decides to take the test, turn to page 21.

If he doesn't, turn to page 112.

Listen guys, fill me in on it at dinner." And with that Chris turned and hiked up the hill toward the cabins. He was just about there when he saw Steve emerge from the woods. "Hey, Steve!" he called.

Steve turned and paused. "Hi, Chris."

"Jeff says you were a wrestler in college," Chris said as he jogged closer. "Do you think you might be able to show me a few moves sometime this week during free time? I really want to make the high-school wrestling team next year."

"Sure thing," Steve replied. "Right now, before dinner, I want to check over some of the sailboats at the boathouse for tomorrow's sailing class. If you want to walk down to the lake with me and give me a hand with the boats, we can talk as we work."

"Great!" Chris agreed.

As they walked toward the boathouse, Chris noticed a bearded man jogging up the hill away from the lake. He was carrying a tackle box. He waved to Steve and Chris before he turned off the path into the woods.

"Who was that?" Chris asked, "I haven't seen him around before."

"His name's Nate Sares," answered Steve. "He lives in a cabin next to the camp. He often cuts across camp property when he goes fishing. He just moved here this spring. He's pretty friendly."

Chris nodded as he watched Nate disappear into the woods. *If he was fishing, I wonder where he left his pole?* Chris thought.

When they reached the boathouse, Steve looked over the sailboats while Chris followed his instructions. When Steve was satisfied that the boats were ready for the next day's class, he picked out a sandy spot on the beach. "This is as good a place as any to practice," he said, motioning Chris to join him. "Why don't you show me a couple of the take-downs that you already know?"

After Steve coached Chris on improving his take-downs, he showed Chris a couple different pin combinations.

"Thanks a lot, Steve!" Chris said gratefully when they were finished. "Do you think we could wrestle a few more times this week? I'd really like to work some more on that last pin combination."

"Sure. I'd be glad to wrestle again," Steve agreed. "Tomorrow morning, I'll be teaching the sailing class, but after lunch I'll have some free time."

"Great!" Chris exclaimed. "I'll be ready!"

After breakfast the next morning, all the Ringers of Cabin 8 (except Jake) decided to take the sailing class with Steve. Even though Chris was eager to work on some more wrestling moves, he was also excited to be sailing.

After Steve showed the group a few of the basics of sailing, the Ringers took several sailboats out on the lake. Steve and Jeff took turns sailing with each boat.

"OK, Pete, tighten the sheet," Steve instructed, after

he climbed into the sailboat with Pete and Willy. "That's the name for the rope you're holding in your hand," he added. Pete pulled on the rope, and the sail grew taut as the wind carried the boat along. The sailboat tilted gently to one side.

"Hey, this is neat!" cried Pete as the boat raced over the water.

"Now I want you to try something," Steve told them, bracing himself against the side of the boat. "When I say 'now,' I want you to let the sheet go slack and duck."

Both boys nodded.

"OK—*now!*"

Pete let out the sheet. Everyone ducked.

The sailboat rocked wildly. The boon careened back and forth across the boat. Slowly, the boat steadied itself.

"We've stopped!" cried Willy, looking up at the sail billowing above him.

"Exactly," Steve said. "Anytime the boat is moving too swiftly or if you have to stop the boat in a hurry, just loosen the sheet and duck. Without the sheet pulling the sail taut, the boat will stop."

"Cool," said Pete.

"OK, I want you to tighten the sheet again, Pete," instructed Steve. "And Willy, take the tiller and keep us on course. I want you to learn how to 'tack'—that is, to sail against the wind."

Like magic, the wind caught the sail again and pulled it taut. The boat tilted gently to its side and began to speed through the water. Steve showed Willy and Pete how to zigzag against the wind. They finally sailed back to shore.

Soon the lesson was over and it was lunchtime. After lunch, the Ringers had devotions and prayer by themselves. Then they had a daily cabin meeting and worked on some camp chores. The whole time Jake stayed on the perimeter doing as little as possible. Finally, late in the afternoon, they had free time. Willy, Pete, and Jim headed back toward the boathouse to go sailing and work on the new techniques they had learned. Jake disappeared by himself into the woods.

Turn to page 75.

By early afternoon, the bus had arrived at Camp Silverlake. When Steve Barton, the camp activities director, met the campers and gave out cabin assignments, Jake found out that he would have to be sharing a cabin with the Ringers all week. He had tried to ignore the group since boarding the bus, but he couldn't help hearing parts of their conversations. They had kept bringing up bell-ringing—as if that was a big thrill—and *Jesus! What a bunch of geeks!* Jake thought. Although Chris, who seemed like their leader, was sort of cool, Sam and Willy had been nonstop jokesters, and Pete seemed to know everything. Then there was Tina—and her brother, Jim—who hadn't said much at all. And Jess was pretty shy, too. But Jill, on the other hand—now there was a girl for you: tougher, more mature . . . *and good-looking, too,* Jake had thought. He had been half interested and half disgusted by their energy and enthusiasm. An expert at staying on the fringes of things when he didn't want to be involved, Jake had given the other kids a few threatening looks and they stayed out of his way. Even Jeff Ellers had begun to leave him alone.

It was his bad luck that he would have to spend the whole week in the same cabin with those losers, but he had endured worse. While the rest of his cabin mates trooped happily off to the lake for their swim test, Jake lagged behind on the path.

When he was sure he wouldn't be noticed, he retraced his steps as quietly as he could and slipped into the woods behind the cabin. For a moment, he thought about running away again, but he didn't have enough money and had no idea how to get back to the city. But at least he was certain he could do just about what he wanted this week and no one would care.

Jake walked deeper into the woods. The sunlight faded a little. He heard some soft scurrying in the trees above him. Finally he sat down on a fallen tree. He pulled his cigarettes out of his back pocket and began to smoke.

It sure was quiet here. Too easy to let your mind wander. His thoughts went back to the car and Bill Grossman. *It couldn't have been him,* he thought, trying to remember clearly the face behind the wheel. Tired of straining his memory, Jake tried to force any disturbing thoughts from his mind and let his thoughts drift aimlessly.

Suddenly he heard footfalls. They were slow and deliberate, as if something quite heavy was making them. Hastily Jake put out his cigarette and stepped behind a tree.

The footfalls stopped. Jake realized his heart was pounding. Could it be Bill Grossman? Had he followed him? Jake glanced down the path toward the camp. Should he make a run for it?

A branch cracked nearby. Whatever it was was right beside him! Jake whirled around just as a huge man stepped out of the forest onto the path in front of him! Without thinking, Jake threw a hard punch to the man's stomach and followed it with another. Before he knew it, he was on the ground, struggling to breathe.

"Get off me!" Jake snarled as he continued to kick.

"Enough!" someone roared above him.

Jake was jerked to his feet. He stared up at the angry face of Steve Barton.

"Do you always hit people before you know who they are?" Steve asked angrily.

"It's a good way to stay alive," Jake growled.

Steve let go of Jake's shoulders. "This week, a 'good way to stay alive' is to look before you start swinging. Why didn't you go to the lake with the other boys in your cabin to take the swim test?"

Jake narrowed his eyes and stared at Steve.

"Can't you swim?"

"So what if I can't?" Jake sneered.

"Then you can learn."

"And look stupid? No thanks."

"I'll teach you when the others aren't around. Or better yet, Jeff could get you started."

Jake stared scornfully at Steve. "Jeff? No way."

Steve looked intently at Jake. Jake was squirming inside. What was with this guy? Jake forced himself to continue to meet Steve's eyes.

"OK, you don't have to swim while you're here. But I want your word that you won't go in the lake above your waist during free time."

"My word?" Jake asked skeptically, staring at Steve's outstretched hand with surprise.

"Your word," Steve repeated.

"OK," Jake replied, his hands remaining at his sides.

Steve dropped his hand and folded his arms across his chest. He casually leaned back against a nearby oak tree. Jake stared at the ground and prepared for a lecture.

"What would you really like to happen this week?"

Jake looked up in surprise. "To be left alone," he answered without thinking.

Steve looked at him thoughtfully. "I can't promise that for the whole week, Jake. But you'll have a couple hours of free time every day to be alone. I'll give you a map if you want to explore the woods. And one more thing: no cigarettes at camp. It's too dangerous to smoke in the woods. I'll have to take the pack you have with you. Give any others you brought with you to Jeff when you get back to the cabin."

Reluctantly, Jake reached into his pocket and handed Steve his cigarettes. No way was he going to give the packs in his suitcase to Jeff unless he was forced to.

"OK, if you follow this trail until it forks—" Steve gestured to the path ahead of him—"the left fork curves around and circles the lake. There's a clearing partway around the lake. Do you have a watch?" When Jake nodded, Steve smiled. "Now you can be alone. Just be back by six o'clock."

Jake looked at his watch. It was three o'clock. He really hadn't planned to do anything but waste a few hours until dinner. But maybe a hike wouldn't be so bad. . . .

100

CHOICE ⇒

If Jake decides to hike down the path that Steve pointed out, turn to page 34.

If he goes back to camp and joins the Ringers, turn to page 74.

If he heads toward the clearing, turn to page 29.

I say we go for it," ventured Sam.

"It's pretty far down!" Chris said, sounding skeptical. "And how are we going to keep the canoe from moving forward while we get into it?"

Sam shook his head. "Maybe one of us could dive in and swim."

"I don't think so," Chris thought out loud. "We don't know how deep the water is—and that current looks pretty swift."

"I guess you're right."

Just as the boys were trying to decide what to do, Steve's canoe rounded the bend. He was canoeing alone.

"Did you guys get tired of canoeing and decide that walking would be faster?" he asked teasingly.

"Very funny," groaned Chris.

"We took the wrong fork," explained Sam.

Steve steadied his canoe in the water. "OK, guys, lie on your bellies and gently lower the canoe. I don't want to get too wet!"

Chris and Sam followed Steve's instructions. After the canoe splashed into the water, Steve steadied it while Chris and Sam ran downstream a ways to where they could scramble down the bank. Then they waded back to the canoe.

"The bridge is right up ahead," Steve said. "I don't

know about you, but I'm sure ready for lunch! Race you to the bridge. Last one there washes the dishes tonight!"

Steve started paddling while Sam and Chris struggled to get into the canoe. When they were finally in, they paddled furiously, but Steve was stronger and had too much of a head start.

"Guess we'll be doing dishes tonight," Sam moaned as they finally reached the bridge.

Steve was watching them, smiling, from the shore. "Ha ha! There's no dishes after a cookout," he said smugly, laughing.

Chris and Sam groaned as they hauled their canoe out of the water onto the beach.

As soon as everyone crowded around the beach, Steve prayed and then gave the go-ahead. Eagerly the Ringers dug into the lunch the camp staff had packed. After they had finished and had taken time for a quick swim, they began the afternoon canoe trip back to Camp Silverlake.

THE END

If you still don't know who the Silverlake Stranger is, turn to page 70 to go on another adventure with the Ringers.

Or, turn to page 121.

We're gonna crash! Yeah!" Willy shouted.

Thwack! Willy and Jake's canoe crashed into the side of the other canoe, denting it.

"Oh no!" yelped Willy, seeing the dent. "We're in trouble now."

Chris paddled furiously to keep their canoe from turning sideways in the current. Willy took a very shallow swipe across the water with his paddle. Water arced neatly over Chris and Sam, forming a glittering rainbow in the sunlight.

"Why you . . . ," sputtered Sam as water cascaded over his face. Willy's paddle skimmed over the water again and sprayed more over Chris and Sam's canoe.

The two canoes slipped into the rapid current together and were soon floating side by side. Both Willy and Jake were splashing Chris and Sam as hard as they could.

Suddenly Willy grabbed Chris and Sam's canoe and started rocking it. Jake dropped his paddle and gave the extra shove needed to tip the canoe over into the water, sending Sam and Chris overboard.

Sam emerged sputtering, struggling to stand up in the chest-deep water.

"You geeks!" he cried as he battled to hold onto the

overturned canoe. "We'll get you back! Then we'll make you pay!" Sam looked around. "Hey, where's Chris?"

At that moment, Chris surfaced on the other side of Jake and Willy's canoe and, with a massive shove, tipped their canoe into the water.

"Awesom-m-me!" Sam yelled approvingly as both Jake and Willy tumbled into the current.

Willy popped out of the water first and grabbed for the canoe. But the current had caught it, and it was already gliding past Jake.

"Hey Jake," Willy yelled, "grab the canoe, man!"

Jake turned around and snarled, "I've had it with you losers! Get the canoe yourself, black boy!" Jake savagely swung around and waded toward the bank.

Willy froze. His great-grandmother Hattie had told him stories about being singled out for being black. And it happened to him from time to time at school. But he hadn't expected it here, and it caught him totally off guard. Inside, he wondered how he should react. "Remember to be Ringers," Miss Whitehead had always said. But she wasn't black.

"Lose that attitude or it's gonna be a long week, pal!" Chris yelled. Jake paid no attention as he sloshed through the chest-deep water toward the bank.

"What an anchovy!" Sam exclaimed loudly, hoping Jake would hear him.

"Yeah, someone should teach that kid a lesson," Chris said, watching Jake effortlessly hoist himself out of the water onto the bank.

"Are you volunteering?" Sam goaded him.

"I just might do that." Chris stared as Jake walked into the trees by the stream.

Jake cast him a sideways look.

CHOICE ⇔

If Chris decides to teach Jake a lesson, turn to page 11.

If he decides to continue on the canoe trip, turn to page 78.

Anger won out. "I don't need this, Preacher," Jake said. He turned, walked out the door, and headed straight for Cabin 8. He grabbed his duffel and left camp, intent on hitchhiking back to D.C.

Steve sighed heavily and stood in the quiet of the cabin, mad at himself for losing control of his frustration. He had seen so many kids like Jake—that's why he ran Camp Silverlake, to give them a chance to listen to God. At times like this, though, he wondered if it was all worth it. Did the "Silverlake Strangers" like Jake get anything out of camp? For that matter, did the "good kids" learn anything they didn't already know, or decide anything they weren't going to decide anyway?

Standing there in front of the outlet, Steve Barton did not know yet that Jake had left camp. And he had no way of knowing what would happen to Jake. He could only pray and hope that Jake hadn't made his final decision to follow a gang instead of Christ.

Steve suddenly felt tired and knelt down in front of one of the bunks. "Lord," he whispered, "please don't let Jake go. Bring him to yourself. Make him see that he needs you. Somehow, some way, make him turn his life over to you." Steve paused, not knowing what else to say, just letting the wish for Jake continue in a silent prayer. Then,

"Protect him, Lord. Please protect him until he does. In Jesus' name, Amen."

Steve rose to his feet, sighed, gripped the screwdriver tightly, and went back to work.

THE END

To find out more about Jake and what's underneath that tough exterior, turn back to the beginning and make different choices along the way.

Or, turn to page 121.

Kicking as hard as he could, Willy pushed the canoe into the shallows. Then he flipped the canoe over and scrambled inside.

Paddles! he thought belatedly as the canoe began to float downstream. He could still see Jake's orange life vest.

"Help!" he called. "Chris! Sam! Can you guys hear me?" The two had stayed behind to ambush Jessica and Jill, but Jeff and Pete were moving rapidly downstream toward Willy's floating canoe.

"Willy's calling for help," exclaimed Pete, as he and Jeff paddled swiftly forward. "I wonder if he's in another water fight?"

Pete and Jeff's canoe rounded the bend and they saw Willy floating slowly downstream.

"Jake's up ahead!" Willy shouted. "Our canoe tipped. I think he might have gotten knocked on the head when the canoe tipped over!"

Both Pete and Jeff paddled past Willy's canoe as fast as they could toward the bobbing orange life preserver. Jeff expertly maneuvered the canoe beside Jake. Pete grabbed Jake's life preserver and, with Jeff's help, pulled him into the canoe.

Jake was dazed, but conscious. Jeff carefully shook him. "Jake? Talk to me, Jake."

Jake groaned and then vomited.

"Pete, about two miles downstream, another bridge goes over the river. There's a gas station by the road. We'll stop there and use the phone."

"What about Willy?"

"I hope someone gives him a ride. If no one does, at least Steve's canoeing behind us. He'll pick him up."

In a few minutes, they had reached the bridge. Jeff called the camp while Pete stayed with Jake.

"Weren't you scared?" he asked Jake once the excitement had passed. "I'd have been terrified."

Jake mumbled something.

Jeff soon returned from calling. "When we get back to Millersburg, I'm going to teach you how to swim. You freaked me out, Jake."

Jake saw the obvious concern on their faces and turned away. Inexplicably, he felt like crying. But he couldn't possibly do that in front of these two, especially Pete. So he swallowed hard and cleared his throat to choke it back. He opened his mouth to say thanks, but instead just mumbled, "I coulda handled it."

Jeff and Pete said nothing more until a pickup pulled into the gas station's parking lot. "Doug's here to take you to the doctor's, Jake," Jeff said. "You've got a nasty bump on the head. I want to be sure you're OK. We'll see you back at camp tonight, hopefully in time for the cookout."

When Jake had left with Doug, Jeff and Pete went back to their canoe and pushed off once again downstream. They paddled awhile in silence.

"I don't think Jake's as tough as he looks," Pete finally said.

Jeff stopped paddling and rested the shaft against the side of the canoe. "Why do you say that, Pete?"

Pete turned around and spoke slowly, as if he were thinking out loud. "Well, I think he acts tough so that no one will want to be his friend."

"I think you're right, Pete," Jeff commented. "Jake doesn't trust people. It's going to take awhile before he's ready to trust anyone here."

Pete didn't say anything more as they continued paddling downstream, caught up in thought. Pete was learning how to be a friend to someone who didn't want one.

That evening, everyone met back at the campfire spot for dinner, minus Jake. It was hot dogs and beans in unlimited numbers for the main feast, with s'mores for dessert, all cooked on the open fire. The whole gang sat on logs around the warm fire in the cool night, the clear sky overhead and crickets clicking endlessly in the woods behind them. They were almost finished when a pickup pulled into the parking lot. Jake stepped out and walked over to the gang.

"What'd the doctor say, Jake?" Willy asked as Jake joined the group by the fire.

"Everything's cool," Jake answered, smiling. It wasn't the whole truth, but Pete noticed a softer look on Jake's face.

It's going to take awhile before he's ready to trust anyone here, Pete remembered Jeff saying.

Willy handed Jake his marshmallow stick, already

loaded with marshmallows. "Here, you can start with these. I'll get us some more."

"Thanks, man," Jake said, catching Willy's eye for a second before looking down.

"S'mores are the greatest things about camping out," Tina said, licking the gooey remains of marshmallow from her fingers.

"No way. Grilled snake meat is," Sam said.

"Yeah! You wanna catch some?" offered Jake enthusiastically.

"Ick!" said all the girls with a shiver.

All the guys laughed. It was going to be a good rest of the week.

THE END

Turn to page 121.

I can't," Sam blurted out. "You guys go on ahead."

"No, we'll wait . . . ," Willy began, but Jim nudged his arm.

"C'mon Willy. I think maybe Sam would like to be alone with Jeff for awhile."

Sam had the look of a man who's trapped on the edge of a cliff and afraid of heights, with only one way to get down. The other Ringers gave him sympathetic looks and followed Jim's advice. "We'll see you back at the cabin, Sam," Chris called encouragingly, as they headed back up the hill.

"Can I still go on the canoe trip on Wednesday?" Sam asked Jeff hesitantly as they walked out of the water.

"Sure," Jeff responded instantly. "Just wear your life preserver." He paused and gave Sam a long look. "But make sure it's buckled right, OK?"

Sam glanced up, remembering his incident with the Coast Guard rescue demonstration. His life preserver had been fastened wrong and had come off in the water, and he hadn't known how to swim at all. Since then, he had learned to swim, but he had never ventured into deep water again. *How did Jeff know about that?* he wondered.

After a small silence, Jeff said, "Let's swim together a few times this week, Sam. Don't worry about the test. Instead, I'll give you some coaching on some survival techniques. What do you think?" When Sam didn't say anything for a few minutes, Jeff continued, "Everybody's afraid, Sam. People are afraid of different things, that's all."

"Chris isn't afraid of anything," Sam answered immediately.

"Maybe he just doesn't show it," Jeff observed. "Even Steve's afraid sometimes."

"Sure," Sam replied skeptically.

"Why don't you ask Steve if he's ever afraid?" Jeff suggested. "He'll tell you. You know, Sam, when someone's afraid of something, the first question to ask is if there's a reason to be afraid."

"I could drown," Sam said hesitantly.

"Yes, you could," Jeff agreed.

"I thought you'd tell me, 'No chance, 'cause I'd be right beside you'!" Sam blurted out.

"If I told you that, it wouldn't be the whole truth," Jeff answered seriously. "Anyone can drown, Sam—even the best swimmers. There's a reason for your fear. But when you have confidence enough in your own ability and you realize the worst that can happen and what you can do to prevent it, then you won't be so afraid."

Sam was silent for the rest of the way back to the cabin. He took a walk by himself after dinner to think things out. What Jeff had said made sense.

He decided to take Jeff up on his offer to give him some help in learning to become a better swimmer. Sam didn't know if he would be less afraid of drowning or not, but he figured it was the best way to start facing up to his fear. After all, some of the things he wanted to do most

114

involved water . . . like the canoe trip. He'd hate to start missing out on stuff. Jim had said that last year the trip was really great. *I wonder what he'll say about this year,* thought Sam.

CHOICE

Turn to page 70 to find out what crazy things happen on this year's canoe trip.

Chris sprinted into the dining room. As he crashed through the door, all the others leaped to their feet.

"Did you see the thief?" shouted Willy, guessing why Chris had come.

Chris nodded.

Sam cried, "Let's go!" The Ringers started out the door.

"The thief headed down the path behind our cabin. Jake followed him and is marking the path," Chris called after them, trying to catch his breath. "Where's Jeff and Steve?"

Jill turned and pointed to a nearby table. Chris raced over to them. "I think we have a thief," he began without introduction. "Jake and I just saw a man who looked like Nate Sares go into Cabin 4 and take a couple cameras and a suitcase."

"Nate?" Steve questioned, "Are you sure it was him?"

"It sure looked like him," Chris gasped.

"Where is Jake?" Jeff asked.

"He followed Nate," Chris puffed.

Steve stood up rapidly. "I'll go with the guys, Jeff, because I know these woods. Would you call the police? Ask for Officer Walker. Have him send somebody out, just in case. OK, Chris," Steve said, turning to him, "Let's go."

Chris dashed back to the cabin with Steve running behind him.

"He went into the woods right here," Chris gasped, pointing to the path.

Steve looked up the path. "Chris, I want you to go back to the mess hall and show the policemen where to start, OK?"

"Sure," panted Chris.

Steve turned and jogged down the path into the woods, catching up with the others just as the path forked.

"He's heading away from the lake," Willy cried, pointing to a cigarette dropped to the right of the path. The gang followed Jake's marks down that trail, jogging steadily for about fifteen minutes. Willy spotted four more cigarettes along the way.

"We're off camp property," Steve commented, breaking off a tree branch to slash at the briars that had overgrown the trail.

"Do you think you guys are making enough noise?"

Everyone froze and looked up.

"I see you found my markers. Did anyone bother to pick them up?" Jake's voice floated sarcastically down from the tree above them.

"The police are coming behind us, so we left them. Do you know where the thief is?" Steve called out.

"I'll show you," Jake said as he dropped from the tree to the path in front of them. "Follow me." They did.

Sam whispered, "Reporting live here at Camp Silverlake, this is Sam Ramirez with WSAM. Many of you are wondering: Just who *is* the Silverlake Stranger? Is he—"

Jake cut him off with a look. Sam smiled a Cheshire grin and said nothing.

After a few moments, Jake paused at the crest of a small hill and pointed to the valley not far below them. "See that small cabin?" he whispered.

"That's Nate Sares's fishing cabin," Steve said. "Jake, are you sure he went in there?"

Jake nodded. "The thief went into that cabin. I was watching it from the tree until you came."

"What'd he look like?" Steve asked.

Jake described the thin, bearded man.

"That sounds like Nate Sares," Steve said. "He's always been friendly enough. The camp staff all knows him. Are you sure you saw him steal something?"

Jake's eyes narrowed. "What difference does it make what I say? You won't believe me anyway."

"What'll we do now?" Willy asked Steve.

"Why don't Jim and Sam jog back and make sure the police can follow our trail and find us?" Steve suggested.

"Let us go, Kimosabe," said Sam somberly.

"Yes, Tonto," replied Jim, playing along. The two took off down the trail.

Before long they were back with Chris and two police officers just behind them. "Where's the thief?" one officer asked. Jim pointed to the small cabin.

The other officer turned to Steve. "There's a road just beyond this valley. I'm going to radio for a squad car to meet us there. You boys stay where you are."

"I'd like to go with you and bring him along as well," Steve said, pointing to Jake. "He saw Nate Sares take the campers' things and then tracked him here. It could be good to have him along." The officers nodded in agreement.

The four of them quietly crept down the hill to the cabin and moved around to the front door. "Nate?" Steve called. The cabin door opened after a few minutes and Nate stepped outside.

"Hey, Steve . . . what's all this?" he asked as he saw the two policemen.

"Maybe nothing," Steve said casually, watching Nate's face. "But a couple of our campers saw you taking some stuff from one of our cabins."

Nate laughed uneasily. "Kids will say anything, won't they?"

"Mind if we look around?" one policeman asked.

Nate shrugged. As soon as the policeman opened the door and went inside, Nate started running for the woods. Jake tackled him. When they saw the struggle, the Ringers came running down from the hill where they had been waiting.

"This place is full of stuff!" Willy exclaimed as he looked through the open cabin door. In a few moments, both officers were walking away from the cabin with Nate Sares between them, his arms handcuffed behind his back.

"Nice work, son," the policeman addressed Jake. "You sure have a nose for crime and some darn good defensive skills."

As they watched the policeman push Nate into the waiting squad car, Willy said, "I woulda never guessed it was Nate."

"Yeah," Pete added, "I thought it was Jake for sure."

"We owe you an apology," Jim said to Jake. "I'm sorry we thought you took the stuff." The other Ringers nodded.

"It ain't the first time," Jake grunted in reply, feeling a little uncomfortable and yet oddly proud. It felt good to do something right for a change—and have everyone know it. Maybe these kids and this camp weren't so bad after all.

Then a whispering voice broke in on Jake's thoughts, "Yes, you have just witnessed—live—the capturing of the Silverlake Stranger. Our unlikely hero, Jake—What's your last name?"

Getting no reply, Sam continued, "Jake 'he needs no introduction' single-handedly led the cops to the hideout of this innocent-looking burglar. The man had fooled everyone, but not Jake. Reporting live, this is Samuel E. Ramirez with WSAM. Back to you, Will."

"Thank you, Sam. Tell us Jake, how does it feel to be a hero, a man on the side of law and order?"

"You kids are weird," Jake replied, shaking his head and sending everyone into uproarious laughter.

THE END

Turn to page 121.

120

As Willy paused with his hand on the doorknob, he heard the sharp barking of a dog near the river where Jake was. He turned around and dashed back to the river. Before he reached it, he saw Jake stumbling toward him, supported by a tall, black-haired man.

"Your friend is hurt," the man said quietly. "We need to take him to a doctor."

"Sounds good to me," panted Willy. "Do you have a phone I could use? I think I'd better call the camp."

"The phone is in the house. The door's not locked."

CHOICE

Turn to page 44.

A thief, a high-school tough guy, and a gang of Ringers. What do they all have to do with a stranger at Camp Silverlake? If you haven't found out yet, go back to the beginning and make other choices until you do.

As the Ringers explore the woods and water of Camp Silverlake, they'll come upon all kinds of adventures. Read on and see what else is in store! If you haven't been following the Ringers for long, you'll soon learn that these adventures involve their faith as much as their fun!

You can find out more about the Ringers, their adventures, and how they trust in God in other *Choice Adventures!*

122

Sally Marcey is a pastor's wife and mother of two children. She has been creating and writing children's stories ever since her own children were old enough to enjoy them. She wrote Choice Adventure #3, *The Underground Railroad*.

*If you enjoy **Choice Adventures,** you'll want to read these exciting series from Tyndale House Publishers!*

McGee and Me!
#1 The Big Lie
#2 A Star in the Breaking
#3 The Not-So-Great Escape
#4 Skate Expectations
#5 Twister and Shout
#6 Back to the Drawing Board
#7 Do the Bright Thing
#8 Take Me Out of the Ball Game
#9 'Twas the Fight before Christmas
#10 In the Nick of Time

Anika Scott
#1 The Impossible Lisa Barnes
#2 Tianna the Terrible

Spindles
#1 The Mystery of the Missing Numbat
#2 The Giant Eagle Rescue

You can find Tyndale books at fine bookstores everywhere.
If you are unable to find these titles at your local bookstore,
you may write for ordering information to:

Tyndale House Publishers
Tyndale Family Products Dept.
Box 448
Wheaton, IL 60189